THE
REBEL ROSE

By Carol Lee Campbell

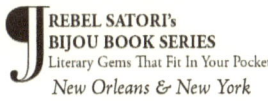

REBEL SATORI's
BIJOU BOOK SERIES
Literary Gems That Fit In Your Pocket
New Orleans & New York

Published in the United States of America by.
Rebel Satori Press.
www.rebelsatoripress.com.

Paperback ISBN: 978-1-60864-278-6.

Library of Congress Control Number: 2024938495

To my daughters, the hope of the Fae

England, 1501

OAK HILL, SEPTEMBER

I can't remember very much. There is a stillness that settles upon me as I lie here, but it is a false peace. Every time my eyes fall shut, red lines appear that flicker and writhe like snakes underneath the skin. Tremors flash dire warnings of lightning that is about to strike. Almost as disarming is the absence of the thunder.

The midwife comes and stops the wounds from festering. I am lying on my stomach. She gently dresses my eyes with a warm wash of herbs that smell good and clean. Hers are small touches, familiar. The tendrils of gray that waft by me like pipe smoke are her hair; the soft, distant birdsong is the whisper of her voice. After a time, I grow curious. Where have these wounds come from?

> *The cuts are from the punishment,* Nettie says.
> *Why did I need to be punished?* I ask.
> *They needed to rid the evil.*
> *The evil what?*
> *I know not.*
> *My hair has been shorn.*
> *They claimed that your vanity was incited by the devil.*

Have I ever been this far away from myself?

Something in me knows that Nettie is choosing how much to say because the truth that floats around us is too painful to acknowledge. Dreams strike me with fear but leave no trace, not a single image to carry into wakefulness.

I have been lodging in a strange shelter in the woods that are thick with green undergrowth for a period of days now. There are stacks of logs on either side of me, covered in sackcloth. The woodcutter's hutch. A large black snake moves quickly in and out of the makeshift walls of logs. I am gathered up in blankets even though the sun finding its way to me through the trees is warm. Nettie comes to my side once more. She whispers in her sing-song way like the sound one hears near a streambed in spring. But I remain disoriented.

You have lost a part of yourself. Come back to me, she says.

A memory then, of a wedding gown, never to be worn. The thought of the dark wool scratching at me, stiff, like a turnip sack, I can shoo away easily. But then another image appears. A thief in godly clothes. Anger and accusation. The reason for my punishment. For a crime I did not commit.

A morning comes when the air is crisp, and my mind is clearer. Nettie is not nearby; she must have left to check on her charges around the manor. I am hungry. Why am I not in the infirmary? The residuals of Nettie's ointment on my clothes irritates my skin and sparks the sting of slashes on my back. I wrap myself with a tattered gray shawl as I slowly stretch into a standing position. There is an open sack that contains two fresh apples and a small black pouch. I pick it up and follow a stone path to the barn. There is no one about.

I go inside the double doorway with rust-worn iron hinges. Hearing a noise, I leap in response, tripping over hay bales. It is just one of the geldings snorting in the next stall. I glimpse the quick movement of a barn cat's orange tail. Where is everyone?

Climbing up to the hay loft, I sit to steady myself. Rocking back and forth, listening to the sounds of the early autumn meadow soothes me somewhat. Crickets haunt the woodwork below me. I look out the wide loft door and watch the insects floating among the dots of white and yellow that are the last of the year's flowers. Tree leaves are changing, some fully red and brown, a yielding to the shift in season.

There is clothing laid out flat upon the hay, a young man's clothes. A small sigil is embroidered on the left side of the shirt denoting the stables of Oak Hill. I take off the rags that hang from my shoulders and touch my scalp where Nettie has treated my wounds. I flinch at the tender spots. Instead of tiny braids at my temples, I have only tufts of hacked horsehair.

My legs are weak, but I am no longer dizzy as I was before. The mysterious cuts and bruises on my body cause me no pain now, though the sting of shame keeps me from looking down at my skin. My right eye feels strange. Too much brightness and it begins to tear up.

I take the clothes and put them on. They fit nicely and comfort me somehow. There is also a little cap with a small red feather. The cap itches but does well to cover up the wool storm, the remains of my reddish tresses. I begin to search through the hay. I know the boy who lives here, the young stable hand. Where is he? I lift the haystacks that scratch at my arms and look around, finding small items of little worth. Hidden below the faded cloth of a thin black pillow is a gray coin wedged within a round groove in the floorboard. I snatch it up and put it in the sack.

As I emerge out of the barn doors, a wide cart and a horse with an unkempt mane pass by me. It is now late afternoon. Past the manor house and just at the gates to the convent up the hill the horse and cart have paused. The driver looks right and left, obviously confused about where to go. He sees the white chapel and jumps down from his seat, a long, little bench with a folded blanket atop it. He sees me.

"You there, boy. Come help me. These rugs are for the nunnery."

He has confounded me. My chest tightens at the sight of the old stone building carefully trimmed with ivy around its door frame, the Convent of the Blessed Comfort. Where I, until recently, lived. The man nods at me and begins to move the reins leading the horse up the little pathway on foot.

He called me *boy*.

"The weight of them is heavy. Comes from Londontown." I don't move. "Are you daft?"

I am still trying to contend with too many thoughts but finally force my legs to move. There is a roaring in my ears. We manage to carry the rugs to the convent doors. A young child stares at me as we make our way inside, and I try to keep my head down. He watches, curious, one of the kitchen boys but says nothing. I tremble and run outside when the chore is complete.

I am about to reenter the woods from where I recently emerged when the man from the cart says to me, "I thank you for the help. I had forgotten the Brandeshire Faire is two days long."

Of course, that is where everyone has gone. I practice acting like a boy as I say, "Excuse me, sir? When will you go back to London?"

"Oh, I wouldn't go all the way to London. Not by myself, a'course. These rugs were delivered from London to Exeter."

"Are you to return to Exeter?"

"I pass that way, yes."

"Will you take me with you?"

EXETER, ST. NICHOLAS

Hamlyn A. Clemens, the driver of the cart, finds Exeter to be the warmest of all cities in the kingdom and speaks to me throughout the ride about the compassion of its inhabitants.

I tell him my name is Matthew and he addresses me in a relaxed way. Master Hamlyn has hair only around the sides of his head, especially in the back. It is gray. He was probably a redhead once. He reminds me of an old sailor with leather skin and a nose that looks as though it has been pocked with salt shards and blue eyes that see right through me.

"Now, you could be the poorest of all poor, and you'd still find yourself a place to sup and clean water to drink. At the cathedral, they have long pipes that bring water to the inside of the monastery, and all the people share what is brought from far afield." He pauses and, after time, adds, "Still, it's hard for the mortal eye to distinguish between the sturdy vagabond and the impotent poor."

He is intentionally speaking of such things on my behalf. I sense he knows me. I may have seen him before, especially in those fruitful years, when the woad was thriving. I am, or was, known as Mathilde the dyer. Our manor of Oak Hill, for over ten years, boasted of the intense hues of our dyes that colored English sheep wool. Merchants across the countryside once compared our blues to the rich tones of indigo brought from India.

A memory of gathering woad in late August surfaces and with it, our sing-song chant: *We gather the woad to dye the wool to sell at market to bring gladness to our lord.*

But then the sweetness of that time turns to vinegar by recent events.

You have lost a part of yourself.

I miss Nettie. I feel the pain in my throat and the tears behind my eyes. I rub my face and keep my head down. Hamlyn has done a fine job up until now of not looking directly at me as if I were a skittish colt. Which I guess I am.

I fall into a fitful sleep late in the back of the cart until late in the day. The wheels react to every pit and stump on the earth-hardened road, but gratefully I can drift into nothingness among the empty turnip sacks and straw.

I come fully awake to a voice that drives the birds from the trees. "*CLUCK CLUCK, CLUCK CLUCK!*"

The cart has stopped. I sit up and look around. My back is stiff and one of the cuts feels as though it may be bleeding above my shoulder blade. It stings as I try to pull the shirt away from the skin.

The horse is unharnessed and grazing nearby. We are at the edge of the wood. I can see the tops of Exeter Cathedral in the distance beyond treelined hills. The sound of the clucking is no hen. It is a shrilly human. I barely resist covering my ears. The source of it is a young woman, maybe a year or so younger than I.

She greets Hamlyn with a slow and measured, "Hello, Hamlyn," and then she talks non-stop. My ears cannot abide the quickness of her speech. I hear descriptions of birds and ponder the mud on her clothes. Faster and faster she talks as if the trees and everything nearby is listening. The sides of my head have begun to ache. After humoring her for a while, Hamlyn shushes her in a soft voice.

I sit up in the back of the wagon. She notices me, a smile spreading across her face, and she strokes my forearms with mud-crusted hands. She is barely more than a child yet casts a pungent air about her that is like the stink of a woman's essence such as when one imbibes too much mead and cheese.

"Who are you?" she demands.

"I am Matty." I try to say the words slowly and with a low voice.

"Gads! Your voice is high. Yet you try to speak low,

7

I can tell." In these hours, I have had time to think and question my new existence, but it is as if my ability to form ideas is sitting in a dark room. I cannot yet fully envision the role I'm trying to play. Already, someone has seen through my disguise! I feel compelled to take off my cap and explain everything.

Hamlyn answers for me. He gives a soft, "Isca, now, now."

"Yes, your words are true," I agree and speak more plainly after that.

"You could be in the boys' choir," she says, pulling a piece of dirty bread from her smock and beginning to eat it. The girl washes it down with ale that Hamlyn passes to her. She takes a long breath and looks at me with a sideways glance.

"Sometimes my younger self talks to me. I wrote a song when I was a wee one. I'd forgotten all about it until this year. Want to hear it?" I give a little nod, and she begins to sing a small ditty. She appears enchanted by her song while she softly breathes the words as if it is a treasure she holds near to her chest. "*All is well and shall be well and well enough again.*"

After several repetitions, the chant seems to soothe her. Her speech slows somewhat. Isca hands Hamlyn a couple of pieces of sackcloth like the ones I had been sleeping on. She climbs into the back of the cart and draws uncomfortably close as if waiting for me to pat her like a pup, then falls asleep, her intermittent snoring rising and falling among the birdsong and lowing of distant sheep.

Hamlyn hitches up his mare, calls her Sheba, and

directs us back to the road. I climb up to the bench beside him, and we ride on in silence for a while. He hands me the jug of ale, and I attempt to swallow a large gulp in a manly way. The road becomes wider and smoother as we enter the last league of the journey into the city. I can see the northeast gate, intense circles and lines of black iron. Finally, Hamlyn speaks. "Isca is the milk maid who once lived with a group of women just beyond the cathedral, there," he points. "But two years ago, when the east gate collapsed, she was hit on the head by the bricks of the crumbling arch. And the injury...She is my niece. My sister passed of an illness and well..." His voice catches, and he looks away.

Exeter Cathedral emerges in its finery, the glory of Christendom in the westward glance of English providence, reflecting the golden light of the fading day. My eyes are stinging from the glare. It rises up, gothic towers aiming for heaven's radiance. Tall arches and spires are polished and gleaming. As we approach, it seems to grow even higher, lifted by the breeze of the open air. I feel a rush of excitement as the sights and sounds draw nearer, but the noises almost send me under the cart for how grand it seems compared to my own village.

I have never been to a town this large before, a city with residences fanning away from me up winding hills, merchants with simple shingles lining up along cobbled streets. I come face to face with the smells of the open market: fish and sweetmeats, refuse and sweat. Wooden cages for small livestock and carts of root vegetables are lined against stone walls on the edges of the square. I can see, even from my troubled gaze, the rolling conduct of the day. The sounds of merchants and their barter, the clergy mumbling prayers while walking two by two, the moan of the beggars making bright chimes with the lone pence inside their cups; it all collides alongside the ancient stone edifices that forever make up the market square. Someone is shouting in the distance, imploring a crowd to look and listen, but I cannot tell where it comes from.

My excitement registers alongside fear. The city of Exeter is as promising as it is foreboding. I am ashamed of how I look and the state I find myself in. I'm rendered an infant birthed into a strange new world. Fatigue takes hold of me as I tried to absorb the new surroundings. The light reflecting off of the wet-streaked streets is too bright in contrast to the shadows where people adjourn for the day.

Hamlyn stops near the almshouse. It is almost dark and getting cooler as the light of the sun descends fast. The building is scrubbed stone and light brick with a three-story tower on one end. I have never seen anything like it.

I mutter a *thank you* to him as best as I am able and step down from the seat. But before he drives away, I glance at him and then to the back of the cart where Isca is sleeping soundly. He and I look at one another eye to eye and I drop the tough boy-act for a moment and bow my head in gratitude. He gives me an encouraging smile.

Almost as soon as I walk inside, I see monks in brown robes everywhere. The men are old and young, and they move with purpose. I approach one of them who has keys jangling from his belt. I mumble with my head bowed that I am seeking shelter.

The young monk does not speak to me. He opens the door and leaves before I can ask any questions. There are three beds in the small space, but no other residents for the moment. I collapse upon a cot and sleep like an insect burrowed in newfound soil and know no more for two days.

I learn that I am in a five-hundred-year-old monastery run by Benedictine monks devoted to St Nicholas. I try to remain unnoticed. No one comes to visit or ask me for the reason I sought their hospitality. I awaken late one afternoon on the third day and sup in the refectory. A few of the monks are giving me sideways glances and I begin to worry that I may be calling out in my sleep. Or perhaps they know what I am. I keep my gaze down and my shoulders hunched forward.

The sound of singing fills the halls early one morning: bright, sweet, childlike exaltations. I recall what the girl, Isca was referring to. The song of the boys' choir pulls me from going into a bottomless well of dark memory and the realization that I have been forced to leave my home. The voices rise and fall in various tones, some achingly haunting. They welcome the season while reflecting on the passing of time. Their swells of passion are in tribute to an archangel, Michael.

After a few more days of adjusting to the surroundings, including taking on a chore or two, I grow curious and wander around the cloister. From my view, outside of the dormitory, I can see a cemetery, gardens, and an orchard enclosed within high ivy-covered walls. My spirit immediately calls me to the small trees, tiny rust-orange leaves beginning to gather on the ground in circles among the rows, heralding the advent of the dark season. As soon as I reach the orchard, I take off my shoes to touch the cold earth and dead leaves beneath my toes. It comforts me to do this.

Cold weather approaches, and I am a pitiful thing. I discovered yesterday that I have lice. The holes in my stockings are crusted with blood and dirt. It feels as though tiny pebbles are stuck inside my slippers. The blisters, though, have turned to calluses. Maybe the worst of all the misery is my homesickness. Nettie would submit to none of this suffering. It is a tragedy to me that my only coin is spent on the most basic and dull of human essentials that I have never had to procure in Oak Hill. I wish I could have spent the money on a grander use, but there is no trinket more worthy than a bottle of lavender and clove oil to soothe the itch and suffocate the pest.

My hands are cracked. They bleed every day. The oils soothe me somewhat but too much and the clove tends to burn. There are new dry, dark spots all over my body but I am not at the point of addressing whatever new disease I have contracted yet. All I want to do is sleep and eat.

One of the monks usually keeps watch when the hour is late and so reports on who comes and who leaves the cloister. As Christ's nativity becomes the chance for celebration and for profit, the road is wide with visitors, merchants and clergy arriving daily.

The monk who carries the keys of the monastery takes pity on me and gives me an extra blanket and a pair of hose. I air the infested blanket in the cold wind outside the dormitory for two nights but it is not enough to completely rid the lice. At least now I am warmer at night.

The monk's name is Saul and he has gray hair springing at wild angles to his shoulders, yet his demeanor is youthful, eyes that speak of a devout life. Up until now, he has taken a vow of silence.

His closest friend is Roberto, an Italian missionary. They are good-hearted men and they treat me with kindness and I am easily their brethren. But I am also an imposter and do not stand close to them when they talk amongst themselves in their space of intimacy. They pray together which is a music of its own.

BLESSED COMFORT

This is not the first time I have spent hours with a clergyman.

For years, I lived with the sisters of the Blessed Comfort. It was a place of tampered moss, stone walls, and sullied glass. The women taught me to read and to write but would not allow me to dwell into womanhood unless I took vows or sought matrimony. I stubbornly refused both options, such a grandiose girl I was.

In the abbey, there were no men to stare at, save visiting fat friars. I was never allowed outside beyond the walls, but Nettie was. The midwife of Oak Hill who picked special herbs and hunted mushrooms for the cooks of the abbey, I sometimes imagine, is like the mother I barely remember from years ago. During cold winter nights when we kept near the fire, I learned to feel the roots in my feet when she shared tales of the blessing trees. I felt my legs spring buoyant as she wove stories about the quickest fawn of the meadow. She said it was part of an important tradition, different from the teachings of the sisters of the abbey, to preserve the lore of nature. Her knowledge, she claimed, came from an old friendship with the earth. She referred often to a power that was greater than the mallet or ax. *We inherit this wisdom as womenfolk.* One of her phrases she used as she and I braided garlic and drank chamomile tea was, *Mother Night comes and blesses us by these thy gifts.* I never had a chance to meet *Mother Night*, but I slept well from Nettie's storytelling.

For years she harvested elderberry for use as a health tonic. She shared in secret that the tonic is a gift from the fairies, as fairies are known to cause and cure all disease. I became her helper for a small amount of time which is why Mother Abbess and the other sisters appeared to forget about me for a while.

I called everyone *Mistress Sister*, which at first made everyone curious about me. This novelty of a young girl puffed up like a robin spouting verse. Every day, I begged them to listen to my sonnets that I had composed in my mind in those years before they had taught me how to read and write.

When I turned fifteen they indulged me my wishes, probably believing that I would be more marriageable if I were better educated. Lessons made of letters and words filled in the void of daily duties.

Nettie was the best audience. With her bright round face, like the moon, her gaze lacked the scorn of so many others. She was the only person who I trusted to share my words with. The pages I was allowed to read were usually from prayerbooks handwritten in English or French. The more costly pages, codices of rich vellum, collections of scrolls and other handwritten parchments, were kept locked in a hall of books near Mother Abbess's quarters. Once I was allowed to read from the Book of Hours, so beautiful for its fine gold leaf and rich blue ink.

After a time, I made for myself a little bound volume, old papers held together with wheat paste, string and discarded pieces of books retired to a drawer in the library. In it I wrote simple phrases, scant sentences with crow feathers used as a stylus found in the sun near the outer walls. If the nuns noticed I borrowed from the ink pot in the hall of books, the room others called a library, they did not mention it.

"*I am lightning when we touch; I am rain when the laughter ends.*"

Nettie took a moment and then reflected, "How could anyone guess that the sisters' teaching would give you such food for your spirit? And your wildness…only…"

Mother Abbess walked in, and Nettie quickly added, "And I will infuse a drink with primrose to reduce thy phrensy." Nettie left, bowing with a brief nod to our head mistress.

She began without hesitation. "Pray thee, Mathilde, you will suffer in this life without a husband." I answered with an utterance that did not meet her standard.

She continued, "We should have had you married years ago. There is a gentleman, a good gentleman, who lost his wife last year. He has children and a farm. A wonderful place for you to begin your life."

"Please, Mother. My servitude is with my sisters."

"You are already past a marriageable age and you refuse the vows of ordination. We were not strong enough to bind the carnal desire that fuels your tongue." She could see my anguish but didn't stop the thrust of the dagger to my heart. "In a fortnight, you will wed. Tomorrow, we will begin the fitting for your gown. Good night, and God keep you, child."

The hallways of the convent were always cold; there were drafts everywhere. My room had no fireplace, so sometimes I slept on the floor with the dogs. My hands always felt chilled and callused. I grew resentful and began taking candles beyond my allotted share.

When I was caught sneaking food from the kitchens by an elder, she told me I was possessed by the devil. But Mother Abbess offered me mercy. I couldn't quite understand this. Days later, she brought a scribe, a friar from the north who looked at me as if I were a great bewildering sea.

Mother Abbess said, "Brother Andrew, this is Mathilde. She is to be wed in a matter of days. You might be the only one to deliver her from her lunacy. Mathilde, Brother Andrew reads and writes much. He has taught young men to read and write. If you are in your proper compliance and obey us as we prepare you for your marriage, perhaps he may offer you advice on your poetry that few enjoy the privilege of."

He glanced at me while addressing the abbess, "Please God, I will help the child if I can." I pretended to gaze at the sky through a small window.

She left. He said to me directly, "Hast thou heard of the famous French queen's sponsored work, *The Art of Courtly Love?*"

I could no longer ignore his presence. I looked over my shoulder at him. Trying to sound unimpressed, I said, "Eleanor of Aquitaine, everyone knows her. *True love joins the heart of persons so that they do not long for anyone else.*"

"Ah, you have heard."

"I contemplate these arguments, but I don't agree with all of them."

"What does thou draw against?"

"The declaration that jealousy is part of true love."

"Maybe you haven't been in love before?"

"Have you?"

Brother Andrew couldn't stop smiling, which didn't bother me, but I wouldn't let on. He added, "Perhaps jealousy is a feeling that turns to monstrosity when it is unrequited."

Replying as shrewdly and as quickly as I could, referring to the only other author I know, I said, "Chaucer has a more accurate invention. *Friars and fiends are seldom far apart.*"

"So, does that mean you are the fiend?"

"Fair point." And then the lines were dissolved between us because I no longer wanted to play games. I wanted to write. "Brother Andrew, why can't I remain in the abbey?" If he will challenge me in prose, I will challenge him my bondage, I thought.

"That is not necessarily what God has chosen for you. Perhaps there are destinies unseen by any of us that invoke the grace of God."

"Can you defend me?" In other words, could Brother Andrew be my savior and help me avoid matrimony that will bind me to a life I did not want? One of the nuns of the Blessed Comfort told me about Christine de Pizan, the French woman who was first a copyist of manuscripts and then wrote books to support her children, mother, and a niece after her husband died. I saw no reason why I could not pursue such an exciting life. Never mind that her father had been a member of King Charles court.

"I will help you as I am able." He says, words with no promise.

"How?"

Brother Andrew said, "Compile your poems, child, and I will oblige thee."

I realize now I have been gullible to those who would befriend me. But when you find another in this life who would listen to your words and speak to you as if they see the ruby in your throat, how could I not trust?

I shared my strings of words with him in the days that followed while my gown was made, the nuns circling me like dancing moths attracted to the weighted brown wool. Nettie was a part of the nuptial planning, imbibing me with her tonics. She spun around me in merriment. "What a miracle that the good gentleman wants to marry you. All will be better for it. It will be a bridge from your troubled circumstance to a happier life."

In my mind I continued to plot other destinies, though I pretended to follow everyone's wishes for me. I had caught a glimpse of the gentleman bachelor once. Twice as old as I and ugly as a goat, I had no intention of marrying him. I decided to get as much out of my meetings with Brother Andrew and when my wedding day arrived I would make a choice about my future.

A week before I was to marry, Brother Andrew told me he would like to offer guidance and suggested I write more pious prose. He said if I brought up a suitable topic to write about, he would be my instrument for godliness. "I have quill at the ready, daughter." He put the narrow-pointed feather in the inkpot.

I thought about it and began. "I shall soon become a Ladywife. I seek the courage to be suitable for my husband."

Nettie nodded. "This is goodness. Your lord will abide by this."

I spoke as clearly as I could. "*I would that God's rapture come upon me when my courses have run clean.*"

Brother Andrew was predictably outraged. "What? I

can't write that!"

"Let me start again."

"Mathilde, you are teasing me, a man of faith who acts in earnest at your summons. But you— "

"My apologies, Brother Andrew. Why would it be a crime for me to speak these words of wellness as the entreaty of the fertile wife? It is well known that the great masters of Roman medicine have imbued their libraries with higher knowledge of when it is best for the ladyship's chance for conception. If they can speak of this, why can't I?"

I could not tell if Nettie was horrified or stifling a laugh. In reflection, I believe she was horrified. Who was I to be so vainly disrespectful to a member of the clergy? Perhaps it was anger masked by childish rebellion. If it were one of the nuns, I would have been punished. But for some reason, Brother Andrew did not summon seriousness or fear.

"Where did you hear this?" He looked a little queasy.

"I listen to the friars talking when they counsel barren women."

After some time and probably with an added prayer for patience, Brother Andrew said, "Speak to me your words, and then I will be the heir of their fitness."

"*Is this what ecstasy looks like? The moths that circle the light from out of darkness find their way, a harmonic convergence of joy and desire.*"

"I will commit to its refinement." He took his time, the coot, and of course he bludgeoned it. Other nuns of the order had wandered in. "Here it is: *Is this what God looks like? The faithful who circle the garden pathways ease their way toward a harmonic convergence of God and His church."*

The nuns in attendance clapped at this great success, the passing of my words of passion into meal stuffs for the pigeons to peck at.

I told him the details of my little bound book of which that most recent passage was a part. Before leaving the abbey for a visit to Rome, Andrew said, "Let me take a look at your book." I brought it to him, beyond thrilled that he wished to see it. He glanced at one or two of the soft, thin pages and peppered me with questions. "You wrote this? Who did you write them for, Sister Mathilde?" So curious he seemed, I was taken aback at my good luck.

"I love all of nature. It calls to me, and my heart answers."

But instead of asking me to recite more words bound within the mismatched sheets, he set it down, gave a quick nod and went about some other correspondence duties. He did not look at me again as he dipped the goose feather into a pot of ink. I began to sputter that I didn't want to leave my book with him. It was mine, with empty pages yet to fill. A nun's attention was caught by my sullen voice and she ushered me out quickly.

Two days later, Brother Andrew departed from the abbey. I returned to the small side chamber where he had spent time working, the self-same desk where he'd placed my book. But there was not a quill or page to be seen; the desk was clean. Where was my book?

I ran like a crazed bird from room to room, looking for my pages. The keeper of all my desires and deepest feelings. Confidant of hope and fears. There was nothing but the stone walkways, emptied friar's chambers and nuns startled from their prayers by my agitation.

I went to the kitchens. There were dead geese stripped, hanging from hooks in the ceiling. Wrung out and prepped for tomorrow's meal. I saw myself in their raw, red-gray exposition. There was a long knife on the table beside the turnips. My deed was nigh. I was crying large tears upon my shift. *My life is ending*, was all I could think. *All my work, gone.*

"I am blindfolded by this passion. It is a sickness of mine – no, it is a plague upon the earth. Why must I be denied my desires and be penned up like the chicken and the sheep? I will not fall to this!"

I cried out as the blade met my flesh. The gray point of it pierced my temple. A perverse covenant with myself. I stopped just as the point of the knife broke the skin. I knew my fate was far outside of my own control. I dropped the blade where it rang loudly upon the stone floor.

But the next morning, I spotted Brother Andrew! On the little lane below me outside of my window. He must have spent the night attending to the lord of manor or one of the resident merchants. I yelled and waved but the glass pane kept me from getting his attention. I watched as he went to the barns to meet with the footman to gather his horse and carriage.

I should have stayed in my room and prayed for peace. I wish now I hadn't responded so impulsively. I should have allowed myself to be married and continue to write a new collection of verses in the privacy of my future matrimonial state. *God's nails*, why did I ever let the tender string of words find the written page?

I confronted him as soon as I reached the entrance of the barn. Brother Andrew responded with indignancies, calling me horrible names and threatening to call the constable. Mother Abbess was already walking out to meet him in answer to his distress. He pointed his finger at me, claiming that when he entered the barn, I was waiting for him in the horse stall, half undressed. As they dragged me away, I shouted obscenities for the venomous liar and thief that he was.

ST. NICHOLAS, DECEMBER

In my new residence I wish to have no contact with any of the monks except for Roberto. Roberto is not interested in advancing through the ranks of authority nor participating in the public pageantry of the church's exaltations. His true passion is the orchard. His talk is of apples. He tells me of his waking dreams that are prayers for next year's abundance in the gardens, even referring to the invocation of Abunda, much to Saul's disdain.

He speaks of the tree's pink petals, a uniqueness found only within a certain week's time in the month of May. "Like tiny angels' wings, the blossoms that spill from the branches, they rival a fairy's beauty." His yearning for the orchard's fruitful resurgence in the summer months speaks to my own desires for the year to turn and for the green to come again.

One cold and gray afternoon, we share in a commonly

known ritual of placing dry bread in the branches of the trees and pouring apple remnants on the ground to bless next year's bounty. He says there are some who beat the tree with a stick to expel the demons dwelling within the trunk, but he could never abide such practices.

I find the men in their brown robes a welcome friendship, although maintaining my distance is becoming more difficult. We break our fast together, first only intermittently but after a few weeks I join them every morning. They sense this but remain polite and treat me as God's willing subject. They have provided me with brown robes and I've accepted. Though they may believe I am considering ordination, I believe it better conceals my body.

Saul includes me in the discussion of Twelvetide that will soon be upon us. He tells me of the singers performing in the refectory on the eve of the feast of St. Silvester, the hall which I only went to for meals when I first arrived in Exeter. They speak of the subdeacon who is vying for revelry, which includes choosing a Lord of Misrule.

Roberto believes this tradition is important for the peasantry. Lives so despairing in poverty must have an outlet for tomfoolery and nonsense. Saul believes that the custom should be outlawed since its origins are pagan. They ask me what I think and I laugh for the first time since coming to Exeter.

They look at me curiously. They genuinely want to know my thoughts. I straighten my spine and say, "What would this lowly sufferer know of authority's wisdom?" When they sit for a lifetime waiting for me to continue, I finally say, "God guides us toward all things on the path to heaven. He already knows where we stand and where we are headed. Simple revelry cannot deter from this."

Roberto is the first to speak. "Ha! Matty chooses predestination."

I reflect on the new nickname while the men look to each other, speaking an unspoken language. Saul leans in across the long table. "Not necessarily. Tradition does not mean absolutism."

I don't understand their argument. It takes me another moment to realize they are referring to me. Roberto laughs. "A heathen in his heart! Or he is a humanist."

Saul scoffs, "Same thing," and changes the subject. "I heard the wandering scholar comes by Epiphany." A small commotion, then – they are excited by the prospect of this.

"To speak or to stay?" asks Roberto.

"Both, I'm told." I am further confused as the conversation shifts to the preparations and foods that will be needed to ensure the quality of the visit.

I lift my sights to the happenings of the church thereafter. Saul directs me to where I may help in the kitchens. Most days I spend there now, cleaning and chopping vegetables for the large pot that will feed more and more people of the city. Saul whispers to me that less interest is shown in many cities for the welfare of the individual. He prays daily for Exeter's continued love for all its peoples, beggar and mayor alike.

The hurt that I have avoided since coming to Exeter feels exposed like a wound that will not heal. How can one's heart remain hardened as ice when the friends around you share their warmth unconditionally? Every day, I sense that they know I am not fully myself, in heart or in dress, and yet they love me anyway.

My friendship blooms with the monks of the cloister and I feel the pain of what happened to me reimagined over a period of days. Things that were nonthreatening to me before all create havoc in my heart now. Sometimes I see a black dog in my dreams. It growls and growls. It will bite my hand if I try to reach for my beloved book. I wake wishing for vengeance of Andrew and the Mother Abbess who stood by while I was beaten for confronting him.

I sit outside my quarters and watch Roberto pruning the berry bushes with his blades. Today is the first of unseasonably mild days with a blue open sky. Roberto informs me that it is the best time to trim the fruit trees and bushes for summer growth. Sometimes, it takes two summers for the full bounty to resolve, he notes while sawing intently back and forth on the oldest branches. There are birds overhead attracted to the bustle in the orchard. By the later part of the afternoon, I spy two bats circling above Roberto when he is aloft on his ladder.

As the hours of the year fall more into shadow, I notice there is no longer a song in my heart to write about. I look down on the streets over the walls where the light of the day slants low in the sky, and only the edges of the town see sunlight. Men and women, now shades of brown and gray, pack their stalls for home. Torches and candles alight everywhere. I hear the soft plainchant of people singing in honor of the virgin. I am tearful from the memory of such everyday actions that herald the start of Oak Hill's midwinter revelry: the hanging of the greens, the stories told by the fireside of Winter Jack, and the cascade of dancing at the year-end festivals. I return to my room.

Saul is soon at my door. He calls, "Matty, come. Roberto has fallen."

I try to quickly clean off my shoes. They are pocketed with holes, and the mud has collected in the edges of the seams. They squish as I step.

I follow Saul, passing the wide doors of the rectory where the great hearth now holds the yule log that must dry for a month's time before being lit. What I suppose I smell is the burning of old kindling below the massive oak to dry it more rapidly.

Exeter's infirmary is a wonder. Nettie would be impressed, too. There are twelve beds, for the twelve apostles. Four monks tend the ill and injured. One leaves as Saul and I approach, nodding to Saul. Roberto smiles at me, and I see the red streaks on his leg above his ankle, which has been bandaged. They have bled him and probably applied a host of presumptive godly acts that Nettie would scoff at. There is charcoal residual with words and symbols of Christ etched below the knee.

Saul looks at me and says quietly, "He fell from his ladder."

I look to Roberto. He is perspiring. He is agitated. I

27

can see he is wrestling to keep his calm demeanor.

"They told me the swelling should lessen before I walk on it again, so here I sit like a toadstool while preparations are made for our esteemed guest."

I lean on the edge of his narrow bed. Saul says, "He is delayed. They sent word. You do not recall?" Roberto responds with a quick shake of his head. He blinks, confused.

He tries to adjust his comfort by punching the cushion under his head. "Perhaps you have only told me that so I will not be concerned while everyone else does my work."

"Who is the esteemed guest?" I ask.

Roberto and Saul each wait for the other to answer. Finally, Saul says, "The wandering scholar is the renowned Salvator Benedictus, a great priest and learned humanist. A follower of Desiderius. His work urges the human quest for a peaceful coexistence."

Roberto adds, "*The most disadvantaged peace is better than the most just war.* What is the reason for the delay, Brother Saul?"

Saul shrugs. "I know not. The weather, his health. He comes from London to visit our shining western city and who would know how he prioritizes us if the pope has called him home?"

Roberto says, "Or if the king would beg an audience."

I am astounded by such associations. "He must be very great."

"Hopefully, you will know soon enough." After a pause, Roberto pats the chair nearest the bed. "Sit beside me, Brother Matty. Tell me a story."

Before I can stop myself, I say, "Must it be of our lord Jesus, or can I summon another tale?" Saul huffs and walks away, but Roberto smiles at my indulgence.

I speak of the lore of Arthur, king of Britain, who had a half-sister that knew magic. He had a wife that loved another. Arthur was a just ruler and earned the sword Excalibur, which was offered by the Lady of the Lake, who also happened to be Lancelot's mother. A sword that was prophesied since before his birth. I sit more deeply in my chair, satisfied to conjure memories of the legend, for this time of year is Arthur's birthing time. He was a Solstice hero who, every year, became the Oak King.

"Spare your brother, Saul. He is troubled by the pagan ways."

"How else could mankind revere the gift of adoration without the sparrow and the orchard? For the light of God shines through nature as well as heaven."

"Why, Brother Matthew, that is beautiful. You are a poet."

"I am lowly born."

"The church would send you to school. Tell me more of the unity from the spirit of the green to Christ's eternal, everlasting light."

"I wonder often what will be left of the Green Man or the Blessed Ladies. To tether them into notions of fancy forgotten for all their sacred virtues, now left only to children's rhymes?"

Roberto reflects on this. "You would make important contributions to our studies. Clothing and food are not the only things that make a man a son of God."

29

"You are the only one I tell these passions to." It is true.

Roberto gazes into my eyes. But a furrow to his brow intrudes, and a roundness to his gaze appears that I have never seen before. I cannot tell if he is in pain or if it is something more, a shadow across his heart. I am no healer but I sense whatever illness approaches will reveal itself soon. I return his gaze with sympathy but sit up straight when I feel a cramp low in my belly that I have not felt in months.

Roberto glances toward the floor near my feet and says, "Matty, your leg is bleeding."

I look down at the trickling red vein stretching down to my ankle. I stand up at once, flippant, dismissive. "I shall go dress this wound gotten by my carelessness while cutting wood yesterday." I walk away as quickly as I am able.

Confounded courses. I have not bled since arriving at Exeter. I have lost weight, though, which has helped to conceal my breasts and has made my monthly blood irregular. To be truthful, people see what you want them to see. I have been walking with my shoulders somewhat hunched forward to keep the outline of my breast from showing through two mantles of monks' wool. I will have to restrict my food intake. Difficult, though, as cold as it has become. Already, I am hungry all day long.

I run to the edge of the River Exe, a blue sky framing the murky green depths. A cold wind stirs off the waters, where abandoned buildings of stone and blackened brick, all windowless and doorless, open through a path flanked by dried rushes. This is a place unused for laborers since the plague took so many from us. The birds are everywhere. The gulls, which normally would invigorate my spirit, are loud and raucous. I peer over the waters and see my reflection in the murky green deep.

How my beauty has deserted me, how wretched my hair and my skin. The winter makes war with everyone's vanity, but mine is like one hundred hits to the head. I realize my new friends care for my soul and not my face. There is comfort in that but also horror. How long will I pretend? When can I grow my hair beyond my shoulders again? When can I perfume my arms with richly scented oils to soften these cracked fingers with salve?

I lay in bed, feigning illness during the week. My fellow bedmates have moved on, for which I am grateful. I had horrible dreams of leeches and snakes clinging to my thighs and my hips. After the third night, I removed the blood-stained bed linens and pondered how to sneak them out of the room and, more importantly, how to clean them. Oh, how often women's tales are dictated by the red that runs. The Rose of Sharon betrays our most intimate privacies. With it comes the knowing that my guesting at the monastery in the likeness of a boy will not last forever.

They let Roberto go back to his room days later when putting weight on the foot did not cause him to grimace. The other monks tease him about his absence from his daily tasks. Something continues to have me doubt

31

Roberto's wellness. There is a shadow between us. His mannerisms are different; he avoids eye contact with me, something he'd never do before the accident. His slight limp is more affected after supping and it adds to his agitated state.

Roberto joins us in mid-December when we eat special cakes on the feast of St Nicholas. He crouches as close to the hearth as he can get, swaddled in thin blankets. Everyone in the rectory shouts with glee as we pour salt and ground copper over the logs that cause the fires to turn miraculous hues as if Belanus himself has arrived to remind us that the spark kindled here in the wood is like the spirit in our hearts that will never die.

They ask for a song, and someone shouts, "Let Matty sing! He has the voice of an angel." I wondered how they know this, but I suppose someone has heard me singing at Nocturns. In the middle of the night my voice is not troubled when roused from slumber much unlike some of the other monks, especially the senior ones who sound like frogs in the night. For the occasion, I sing the Christian version of a ballad called *Greensleeves*.

In the midst of song, I look to Roberto, huddled alone by the fire. I smile at him and he begins to cry. I try to utilize my singing as a prayer for him. He only hangs his head, seeing and hearing something invisible to the rest of us.

The next day, I hear shouting. It is Roberto's voice calling for me. When I run from my room, I see him come towards me as if he were a drunkard in the halls, blankets trailing behind him like seaweed from a ship. Dark circles surround his eyes and his face is pasty-looking. Fellow monks and novices appear, rushing to his side. I fear some violence will follow.

I grasp his arms and hold him. "Come, let us to the orchards though they be sleeping, my friend." He seems to falter, trying to remember what I speak of, but then follows me. Everyone else returns to their work, but several glances linger in our direction. They have a feeling, as I do that Roberto's troubles are nigh, and in no quick time will they be relieved.

Outside, we pull cloaks and blankets tightly around us. Snow falls slowly, and flakes are whispers of tiny worlds not yet born.

"Matty, oh Matty."

"Roberto, when did you last sup?" I steal a glance; his head is tilted sideways.

"Matty, my head is full of hornets." He grabs at his face and sways back and forth. I think to myself, I will go to the kitchens and search the wares for herbs to calm him. It won't cure but it is certainly how Nettie has kept the lords and ladies of Oak Hill calm in their anxiousness. Though, with another glance at Roberto, I know these efforts will be in vain.

He looks at me with clear eyes focused on the whole of my face. "Matty, I must show you something." He sits at an old stone bench and uncovers his ankle. The punctures are mostly closed but framed with puffy red lines. It is a bite of some kind.

Bats.

I sit down beside him, and Roberto begins to weep.

He leans against my shoulder and we both pray together through the morning while the cold sun peaks through fast-moving clouds. I am reminded that humans are helpless to the desires of fate.

I stay with Roberto. I am released from some of my duties. He tells me in a lucid moment that he knows who I am, what I am. I weep more from relief than worry. He tells me I look more beautiful now than at any other moment because my face is not hiding who I am. He grabs my hand and holds it tightly. "Never forget who you are, Matty. Even when you must pretend."

The next day, Roberto reminisces for a few calm moments about his family's home. His father's parents both worked translating Greek philosophy into Latin and were employed by the Medici's Platonic schools. Roberto grew up in the village outside of Rome where young novices were recruited to spread the word of Christ in England through missionary work. Of course, I've already heard much of this, but I let him talk. It seems to distract him from his pain. After a time, though, his mouth fills with saliva. I offer to bring him water. He gives a wan smile and declines. When I bring him a cup later, he shakes his head, and I watch as he glances at the cup with something akin to revulsion.

Saul shares with me later in the evening that Roberto's fear of water is a disease that causes saliva production to greatly increase, and when a man attempts to drink, it may cause excruciatingly painful spasms of the muscles in the throat. Poor Roberto.

"How long will he suffer?"

"I do not know."

EXETER, JANUARY

Salvator Benedictus finally arrives after Epiphany. He spends time wandering the markets in central Exeter with his entourage of guests and a group of our monks, praising the great generosity of our work and the magnificence of the cathedral.

He speaks in public houses during his stay and only in the cathedral once. Every talk he gives, he has something different to say. Is he trying to keep monks happy in their fashion in church while entertaining the wealthy merchants of Exeter in the taverns with different words?

With a contingent of monks and laymen of different ages and stations, we listen to Salvator speak one cold night at a merchant's house near the market. The fire in the hearth and the people gathered instill a warmth about the place.

He says, "Greetings, good fellows, all of you! I have much gratitude for your invitation to visit this beautiful city in the western glory that is England. I want to tell you about my current deliberations. My most recent works are inspired by a friend here in England, John Colet. I soon hope to print a publication I will call *The Reason for Peace*. I say to you, I am fearful for my mother church in Rome. Our rulers must strive to fulfill their obligations by speaking against war. They must preserve Christian harmony, not through the acts of suppression or by forceful authority.

"Rulers, care for all of your people. We learn this from the Greek philosophers from one thousand years ago but we do not heed the edict. Rome needs to be the center of reform for its cruel practices. For its greed. Make Christ's words available to every commoner who wishes to read it. This will not upend the church, but rather, it will fill the sails of every soul who seeks God, and then they will know Him. I swear it. People will do the right thing in godliness if they have access to the keys of Christian liturgy. I am sure of this."

Occasionally, people pound the table or applaud. How can this man be a proponent of Greek and Roman studies and yet still be a priest leading sacrament? His convictions show a greater understanding, a larger picture in the world of literary accomplishments and, as he called it, the philosophy of Christ.

The next day, I return to the infirmary to sit beside Roberto who again is refusing food or drink. I remember the sleeping seeds from the black pouch that was Nettie's. Do I still have them? I run to my room and sift through the old bag. Yes, thank goodness, and after several prompts, Roberto accepts one, though he cannot swallow it. It mostly dissolves on his tongue. While he is asleep, Saul helps me open his mouth, and I pour broth into his throat, a tiny trickle at a time. Sometimes, he can't swallow and coughs it up. But we are able to get some nourishment into his body. He sleeps so deeply other monks are concerned he may have passed on. I hold my breath through this waiting but, thankfully, he wakes the next morning. He appears calmer as well.

Which is fortunate because into the infirmary walks the abbot and Saul with Father Benedictus. I learn later it was he who requested to see how the sick and injured fare in the grand infirmary of St Nicholas. Benedictus, for his part, wears a handsome coat, lined with something that looks like beaver fur. He also dons a matching dark square hat with a coif. I try not to stare as I imagine the warmth enveloping his shoulders.

"Salvator, friend, come to Roberto's bedside and comfort him," asks Saul. Roberto immediately tries to sit up to welcome the city's most honored guest but he is suddenly frenzied, the water glass next to him appearing to terrorize him. I move it away. Roberto's eyes fall to me. He calms again, trying to hold on to his senses for a minute inside the space of chaos's storm.

"My dear Father Benedictus, I am humbled by your presence here." He falls back against the pillows, perspiring. He steels himself again. "Sire, you must meet my friend, Matthew. He is come from other parts of Britain, and he is one of the most..." and then he pauses, not finding the words. "Matthew is a bridgebuilder helping wandering souls understand the multitude of goodness of works by those of older faiths that may be rest assured their philosophy alights within the magnificence of Christ." At first, there is too much silence. I fear Roberto does me a disservice and disrespects his order. Salvator gives a little smile and a quick nod. A darting glance to me and then a few compassionate words to my friend.

Roberto chokes on his spittle, and we move away from the bed as to not excite him further. Saul ushers me to join

37

with them as we leave.

We go to a tavern to sup. There is dense bread and more than one kind of beer. There are lamb shanks and the last of winter root vegetables roasted in pig fat and brine. I sit quite still in honor of the feast.

Salvator looks at me. "Tell me, Matthew, what was young Roberto referring to when he spoke of you in such high regard?"

I try to shake my head, but his studying gaze is fixed on me, a disciplined instrument replete with all of God's patience.

"I would like to pretend he speaks from illness, but in truth, sire, we have shared a lifetime of conversations about our love of all nature." After wrestling with my thoughts, I decide to speak plainly. "The stirring of springtime is as sacred to me as is the Word. These are God's gifts to us, my lord."

The others are quiet. I knew they would be. Saul will judge. I say, "My life before the introduction to the monastery was in farming, sire. Tending the soil and the growing things. This cultivates wisdom, not to mention the means to our very survival."

Benedictus nods. "All sound secular learning is godly learning. We cultivate the soil, and we cultivate the soul. My parents both died of the plague." Here, he crosses himself." So many people thought everyone would die, especially the plague that doomed mankind. The world has become so fearful. My parents were good people. My mother used to tell me stories that remind me of your words. Hers were stories not always aligned with God but with goodness. She used to tell me that she believed she conceived me after she drank water from a special well and ate of salmon that tasted of ambrosia. Hah! We may laugh at these things now. Some of us may judge. But young children, and the child that remains within our own breast, needs such tufts of spirit."

He has broken my distillation of what I thought a man of God could be. Yes, I am going to follow this teacher if he will lead me. My heart is full with the possibilities of learning.

One night, in yet another tavern, I dine with Salvator and his friends. As the evening finds its end, he leans forward to speak directly to me. I don't let him get too close for fear of him detecting the truth of my womanhood. In this light, I can see the silver strands in his hair and at his temples.

The wandering scholar looks into my eyes and extends an invitation to travel with him to the famed Castle of Castile in a country far from here. To the great house of Trastámara! I am to be part of his entourage. This honor swims across my vision like some kind of dream. I hold tight to the arms of the chair as if they were reins of a fast-moving horse. I ignore the scornful eyes of Saul and ponder a future I never imagined before. I will have a lifeline to my writing and be among a company of great thinkers. The world will open up for me. I can feel it in my belly. I nod quickly, worrying that delaying a response will give him the chance to change his mind. He knows of my concern for Roberto and says I may come join him when I choose if he leaves Exeter before I am ready.

The morrow brings no release for my friend. He is shouting all the time. I cannot come near him. He rants at me. The monks have moved him back to his room and have had to tie him down. His mind is gone.

I go to his room to tell him about my visit, hoping and praying for a tranquil moment, fearing I may have to say goodbye to him. Roberto's once soft brown eyes are wild and bloodshot, with a look that pulls me from the news I intended to share with him. He shouts at me, "The Roman of the Rose! Look, there she is, dwelling among us! Father Abbot, men of rank, stop her, though she be a superhuman woman, she will fill our heads with delusions." Through the ropes around his wrists, he manages to point at me and say, "She walks among us! Woman born!" He strains against the ties. I am shaking in my shoes. My heart is lurching in my chest. I turn from him to flee, and I see Saul standing at the door, watching.

Saul mumbles a prayer but the tone of his voice is mocking. He looks at me with dead eyes. "Forgive him, Father. Forgive our Roberto for speaking this way to Brother Matty." I run from the room.

Days later, my courses have started again and I am forced to find a place to bathe unseen. I sneak over to a part of the cloister where I believe I can bathe in private. I need more than wet strips of linen to wipe away some of my monthly blood. The flow is heavy.

I bring a bucket of water to a small area outdoors

surrounded by the walls near the women's cloister. There are women singing. I put the bucket down near the open kitchen windows which give off steam and heat from the day's cooking. I sense I am being watched and take extra care to not be followed, but Saul is craftier than I thought.

He must have followed me and watched me bathe. He would have known that sooner or later, my courses would arrive and catch me as a woman. Saul shouts at me as I shove my meager possessions into a sack and leave the room of the monastery. The new sleep mates evacuate as soon as they hear him. My heart falls like a stone into my belly as I witness how this great revelation in the monastery will affect…everything. I can already sense my plans for Spain evaporating before my eyes. Saul is quick on my heels.

"Roberto spoke in earnest! I knew it. You dishonor all of us! Gather your things and get out!"

I look him in the eye. "I came here, and I loved you all. I meant no harm."

"Born a woman. You are a deceiver. As was Eve. Get thee gone."

"But Salvator Benedictus …" Surely, Saul would not reveal the truth of who I am and destroy my destiny.

"What about Salvator Benedictus? Oh, the *great* Salvator. He is not God's chosen, as you may think. God has His own plans, more than you would know. Salvator's parents weren't married when he was born. The pox punished them for their sins. And why is our monastery still here after five hundred years and will continue to be here for five hundred more? Until the holy Christ comes

41

knocking, we follow our contract with God. So…there you have the truth of things."

It is the last of the dying light of the day as I exit the cloister. My mind is reeling. Where shall I go with only a cloak, a boy's tunic and old shoes?

HOLTSWATER, FEBRUARY

I run from the city, the world I knew for that cold handful of months. Kicking rocks and refuse out of my way, the chatter of merchants and shuffle of crowd ebbs almost as soon as I pass through the iron gates. Small squares of farmland give way to large sloping brown hills curtained by tall skeletal trees in the distance.

I collapse in a wide-open hayfield that is wet and brown and desolate. Late winter casts a gray mark upon me. I fall asleep after exhausting myself with the tears of a toddler and wake up chilled in the dark. My hands are tingling, edging near numbness. Fear looms from my bones about what the night could bring. I look behind me toward the city; lights are blinking from windows like eyes trying to focus. Sounds surround me that I do not recognize. The clank of metals is a ringing bell, like an echo. In the north I can see the fires from encampments further out in the countryside. Probably bands of camp men that are said to linger nearby when they're not thieving. I laugh at myself. For I am a thief.

The first time I stole, I was thirteen. I snuck outside of the convent walls and then found myself locked out. I wandered alone, hiding behind wide trunk trees, reacting in horror for every sound that I heard, even the tiniest snap of a twig. When darkness set in, I came upon a farmhouse. Behind the back door, I found an elaborate table covered in threadbare velvet. Placed upon the cloth were small fruit pies. Food intended as offerings for the fairy folk. In subsequent years, I rejoiced in the secret discovery of foods at auspicious moments of the year when women young and old left offerings outside their doors to gain favor with the spirits that were said to grant wishes for those worthy.

And now, finding myself within the cloak of gray-brown cluster of bare trees, I bed down upon last year's fallen leaves, surrounding myself with the wet, decaying brownness seeking warmth. My thoughts travel to Nettie and the simple life I knew before I came to the city. The tears quickly follow. I release a mournful cry, like the sad song of a bird flying to her nest and finding all inhabitants gone. Sleeping uneasily with my old monk's cloak wrapped tightly, I swaddle myself.

In the early morning hours I can hear small rodents under the leaves making their way around me. I search what's in my bag and find the small pouch of sleeping seeds. I remember Nettie telling me once that to take them all would create in the body a final rest. I place them in my hand.

Suddenly I have a sense I am not the only one who is aware of these creatures underfoot. I glance to the high branch above me. There is a hawk, cloaked in red and brown feathers with a creamy soft chest. When she looks in my direction it is for certain as though she is looking at me as if I am an intruder. But the stirring underneath me causes my breathing to stop. My chest hurts. Why must bad memories surface at the darkest moments?

When I was a child, I spent all the hours of the day that I could in the woodlands. I made masks from the largest, strong brown leaves I could find. Pasted together with flour and water, with peeled-away holes for the eyes and mouth, I tied it to my head with string stolen from the manor. Wandering alone after my mother died, I wore masks to hide my face because it was red and puffy from crying. I think about the masks. In a way, I suppose I still wear one.

I try to keep Roberto's thoughts alive while consider the years long ago when I hid, like the rodents around me. Safe places away from the sun, away from the predator that hunted me.

Never forget who you are, Matty. Even when you must pretend.

BLESSED COMFORT, TEN YEARS AGO

Raymond and I became friends when I was ten. Though he was about three years older, we played hide-and-seek games in the years before his voice changed while he was still a hairless, skinny, baffled youth. There were other children nearby, but Odebury Manor and its surrounding inhabitants had been reduced in size. A tide was turning; many yeoman and laborers decided to go to the cities for a more reliable, and hopefully larger, coin. The convent had maintained its wealth, though, and so was able to remain intact, along with stables that housed twelve horses and two stable hands. One was Raymond.

When he was finished cleaning the stalls and grooming the geldings, we would run to the stream bed to watch the polliwogs in the spring and the migrations of birds in the autumn. The woods were a huge place for us to play; we only had to be mindful of the hunter's arrow or the cook's foraging around us.

Raymond was the only friend who stopped whatever he was doing to oblige me my silly requests. I had enough trust to play different word games. He taught me about the legends of toads, of how they were poisonous when they grew their legs. Sometimes, I thought he was making it up as he went. *It is the legs that are filled with poison, that is why tadpoles have no threat.* But I enjoyed his whimsy; we could make each other laugh. By the time I had gone to live in the convent, I could not tell anything was different about me. Other than my frock was too tight. I had a kirtle made for me and felt quite grown up. Around that time, Raymond said he wanted to play different kinds of games, games, that made my stomachache. He stared at my breasts, and I felt my face turn bright pink. He said he wanted to play our hide-and-seek game without clothes.

One day, he said I should come up with a new game to play. I had heard tales of courtly love held together by beautiful words that bards used to make an audience's eyes light up. They had the power to stave off the hunger in the belly or the sadness in the heart. I said, *Say something that alights the wild inside of us.* I was referring more to the fairy lights that awaken the woodlands or the night owl who sings at the edge of the forest. But Raymond only stared at me blankly, confused. I sensed he secretly hoped for ways to touch me. I discovered that the freedoms we explored in our time together were fueled by different desires, different temperatures in blood.

I asked Raymond, with his indistinct red fuzz atop his head and a tiny bit of rusty yarn above his lip, "Share the words of your heart."

He does not know what I mean. He looks at me as if I wear a headscarf made of snakes. He says, a voice quite anguished, "What do you want me to say?" I stay quiet just long enough and then he utters, "My mind is empty but my heart is full of love for you."

The words fill me with absolute joy, so simple and pure in reticence. I grab Raymond's hands and hold him tightly to me. Then, I see in his eyes that he did not desire simple friendship. He bared his soul to me but I do not feel the same way for him. He knew it. On that day, I learned that I had kindled fire, which fed unintended passions.

It must have been my fault that Raymond's open heart caused him to act differently around me. Our friendship had been nothing but kittens but had now become lions.

I began to avoid Raymond because he scared me, the look in his eyes, the sound of his voice.

One day, I ran back to the convent after Raymond found me near a meadow picking elderberries. I was told by a sister to go groom the horses because Raymond was nowhere about, and the abbess had business in Exeter in the morning. Someone needed to go attend her now. I at first stammered a response but then did as I was told.

Raymond appeared from the saddle room, smelling of sweat and leather. He carried oats to stalls, where a smaller pony knickered. Raymond continued about his business brushing down the neck and flanks, cleaning out the hooves, holding first one leg up and then other. He walked by me and led two horses out the back gate, where they stood at the water basin, tails swishing as the rain came down. He acted as if I wasn't there.

Days later, when I was told to prepare for Mother Abbess's return, I went to brush and braid some of the mare's manes and found Raymond alone in a stall. I began to gently encourage him to come help me. We needed to make the barns look presentable, but he bade me come closer. From the other side of two bales of hay, I could see Raymond's manhood exposed. He was playing with himself. He shouted at me; I couldn't leave until he was finished. Of course, being only eleven years old, I didn't know what he was talking about. He groaned and grunted, and his thin body heaved forward. He wiped his hands on the hay, then wiped his hands on my apron and shoved me away as he left.

And then, one day, he approached me and told me to take off my clothes. I ran from him again; this time I was quick enough to become invisible as soon as I crossed the stream. Raymond called out to me. The only sound was of the bird song, the stream bed which had risen in the week of heavy rains. I found a hollowed tree trunk near the edge of the north hills that bordered a high meadow covered with late summer flowers.

I hid in that tree trunk until dark. The mice came out at dusk and made their way unseen through the briar, through the fern. I blended into the dark of that hollowed tree, where lightening had struck it and killed it two summers before. Where the only inhabitants were large orange capped woodpeckers.

I ran home and was chided for being late. The next morning I begged a conference with Mother Abbess and I told her what happened to me.

Her face was smoothly tucked into the folds of her habit like layers of thick cream, soon to become butter. I cried at her feet, but she only turned away from me.

That was when I found the library. Some parts dusty, old scrolls, some parts expensive vellum held safe under glass or gold-line illuminated scripture, I came to love the quiet. No one was allowed there since it was part of Mother Abbess's private reading room. The room was filled with tapestries and bookshelves and a desk with a wide chair. Some of the bookshelves were built into the walls, some were more ornamental with oak sculpted moldings.

A week or so later, Raymond was sent to live with an uncle up north. I never learned whether or not the Mother Abbess arranged it on my behalf. But the library became my new woodlands to roam. A new place to bide my time unnoticed when the sisters of the Blessed Comfort had begun their long tirade of trying to convince me to marry or take vows if I wanted to remain. A part of me knew, even then, that they felt I had insulted their kindness in helping me to learn to read.

UNDER THE HAWK, OUTSIDE OF EXETER, TODAY

I think about hiding as a child. And here I am hiding again. After some amount of time, I feel as though I am swimming between the past and present. I cannot tell the difference between memories of Raymond and the truth of my own current fate. Everything is happening at once, I force myself to stand up. I decide I will not live as a mouse always scurrying underfoot or hiding in a tree trunk.

The hawk flies away toward the rose-colored clouds of dawn.

EXETER TO HOLTSWATER

The next morning, the wind shifts. Winter's bite has lessened. I can hear music in the distance coming from the city which is behind the woods west of where I stand. It begins to rain, a drizzle that further obscures the sounds of the city. My hair is cold and wet around my cheeks. The felting brown wool cloak offers little protection. I pull my hood up above my forehead.

I remember that festival season has arrived. Perhaps the visitors and residents will share their wealth as they rekindle the new year's commerce. I may beg for a spoonful of broth.

I join with the other early travelers arriving in the city on the road, where the blue and gold pennants above our heads wave and snap in the stiff breeze. People disperse after squeezing through the gates focusing on their own hopes and plans for the day, many moving towards a preferred location to sell their goods. At the top of High Street, the town square requires a constant maneuvering of brown water puddles, but toward the north end, nearer to the almshouse and fountain, it is mostly mud and stone.

In my hungry and cold state, my gaze is worn. I see the gray clouds even though the rain has stopped for now. I see only smeared white and pink makeup on the faces of the Morris dancers, not their nimble feet or streaming ribbons. They are practicing, making ready for a performance. The clacking of their sticks is slow and measured.

I see the bruised and ugly apples in a cart before I notice the wax-sealed tonics in small bottles gleaming like purple jewels. I smell animal dung and spoiled meat, not the buoyant scent of hothouse flowers sold as small posies on a table nearby.

As the sun moves low across the late February sky, the crowds advance. I hear singers coming from near the church – and, thank all that is merciful, there is a breadline with broth! The monk serving is one I recognize from the months at St Nicholas, but I don't think he knows me. Perhaps the line is too long. Perhaps he cannot stand to look at the whole of us who wait and would otherwise go hungry. I get in line for a second helping and am astonished for the additional piece of bread placed into my dirty hands.

Before I turn away, I cannot help but ask, "What news of Brother Roberto?"

The monk is startled from his duties and looks at me plainly. "He has passed to God." Then he pours broth into a wooden cup for the person waiting behind me as I step aside.

Children run from stall to stall, finding impatient vendors shooing them away from their wares, sometimes with shouts, mostly waving at them as if they were flies. I think only of my brother, the Roman child of God. I sit down on the muddy ground close to a building and try to speak a prayer for the one who befriended me when I was lost. I finish my bread.

Pheasant and quail poke their heads through wooden slats from a vendor's cart. They squawk at one another. I watch them in their cages but don't see them. I look around and notice that those with smiles on their faces are perhaps some of the poorest of us, enjoying a day free from endless chores.

A crowd gathers before a large wide wagon which is covered in pieces of felt-like brown cloth, the wheels just barely exposed beneath. A row of Tudor buildings encloses the wagon, which I realize is a stage. Just as clouds have move apart and the sun breaks for a moment through the dullness of the gray sky, two male angels with long-haired wigs enter from a ladder on the back side. They stand inside of an arch and gesture toward the crowd with bell-sleeved arms.

A morality play. I have heard of these but not seen one before. Though it's well passed Candlemas, and near to Lent, we are probably witnessing the enactment of the cleansing of the virgin after childbirth. The men, with long red wigs and flowing white robes, are discussing the grace of God's hand. They begin to sing softly.

People near the stage are rapt, but smaller groups further back chat quietly while keeping one eye on the players before them. There are small groups of nobility too, who draw attention by the brightness of their fur-lined robes and gold adornments.

I wander among two men with strange hats talking with the local baron. The merchants' accents are strange. They sell rugs and spices, rows of little brown glass bottles and earthenware jars have caught the attention of the baron's entourage. With their hand gestures, I can tell they are from somewhere far away from here. I'm tempted to come stand beside them and indulge for a brief instant in the smells of clove and dried orange, but do not feel like listening to the nobleman talk about his privilege.

The baron turns to another man, a nobleman, I believe, called Thomas Howard, an earl with new lands north of here. He, too is a boaster, reminding everyone who will listen that it was to his very home that he and his wife welcomed a red-haired Castilian princess who landed at Plymouth. This is met with a dull response by the baron. Everyone has heard and dissected this news, now half a year old. Plus, I'm told, the royal couple has settled in life at Ludlow Castle in the north. I'm also told that there is no talk of an heir, but sickness instead. No one will say the word, but everyone from peasant to pope trembles at the thought of plague. It remains as present as a cloak in winter.

"She was due in at Southampton, but because of the terrible storms they found the dry land of Plymouth much more inviting. And praise God, we, and all of my kin, with all goodly manner and speedy reception, greeted her when she landed. She stayed with us a full week and brought her entourage of extraordinary creatures…. Moors as servants, walking musicians. Quite the spectacle." The baron moves on with an adieu to Master Howard, his hands full of trinkets and goods which he hands to his servant.

Perhaps it is Master Howard's mention of Spain that makes me think of Salvator. I consider for a moment: Is it possible that the wandering scholar is unaware of what happened to me? I picture a moment in the future; I wear a rich embroidered cloak. And then, in my mind's eye, I find the predetermined place to greet Salvator and my new friends. We smile as we tell the journeys we each undertook to continue our fellowship.

I move away from the noblemen and move toward more merchant stalls perched against the north wall of High Street, where Tudor stripes painted on old stone and wood houses align with the slats of carts and the legs of tables. The road begins to narrow at a cross street, the stones being so uneven I must step with care. My eyes alight on a bookseller's table. As I approach, the mud on my cloak and the Oak Hill badge on my well-worn tunic tells him everything he needs to know. He will not glance in my direction even after I stand there for what feels like an hour.

His inventory includes small chapbooks, cheaply made in dull colors tied through with course threads. Behind him, tucked into small wooden cases, are a couple of stacks of finer books. There is even a small pile of codices made of stitched parchment, including one that could be costly vellum. They are like little jewels of a crown. I'm drawn to them. Behind a few larger tomes printed from a press there are ink pots and quills of goose and swan feather. Oh, and a pen knife. I glance down at my hands, the ink stains of blackish blue long faded.

At the front of the stall are small, newly copied books of parchment, all written by hand. Tender etching of gold and ocean blue sweep the cover and trim the edges of the pages. I notice, too, large tomes printed from a press. But my eye is suddenly drawn elsewhere.

The book, *Joy and Virtues of the Godly Life* is by an author named Angelus Santos. I open the pages midway, such a sweet little book. But as I read, the words become confusing. My heart starts pounding telling me that something is wrong.

It reads, *"Why is there yearning in my heart? Is it a pearl that wanders lost through the pulsing of a body's current in search of God's love? Is it like the pollen to the bee? Does God love them as He loves me?"*

I cannot make sense of what I am seeing. Then, like old friends who come embrace me in long lost memory, I whisper the words I know. *"Why is there yearning in a woman's breast? Is it a pearl that wanders lost, pulsing through the body's current in search of a lover's touch? Is it chosen or is it necessary as the pollen to the bee? They must want of something ineffable as well. Does love please them as it pleases me?"*

I recite the words in defiance of these heinous pages. I almost rip the sheets from the spine. Staring at my own words through this vessel of debauchery is a dagger to my heart, which has shrunken into a raw and useless thing.

Master Bookseller attempts to snatch the book from my hands so we are both holding it tightly, pulling it to and fro. "How well for you that you can read." He spits it plainly as if I am a sullen child. "Are you to purchase the book or not?"

I cannot move. The choking sensation in my throat has paralyzed my limbs. I still cannot make sense of what I am seeing. He barks again, "And now you smear it with your foul tears." He rips the little book, stained now, but only a little as if he has yanked my heart out of my chest. The act sends me forward on my toes, my elbows almost knock over the whole of his set of stacked books that teeter on tables too small. I somehow lean my head back, which helps me steady myself.

Another customer happens by, stops beside me, and picks up a copy of Angelus's book. The bookseller returns to a pleasant demeanor. His face is that of a Janus god, moving from a sneer to a smile. To me, he growls, "You oddly clad, little waif. Get thee gone."

I consider lying down in the street and letting a coach run over me.

I glance at the crowd in front of the wagon. It has widened, and cheering erupts from the performance, measure after measure. I slowly turn away from the stacks

55

of books and the other stalls, the sounds of vendors and their merry, solicitous tone jarring in my ear.

I look once more at the bookseller. *He* is the monster, not me. He is selling stolen works – he is the abomination. But then I glance down at my strange outfit and bite my lip. He has a point.

Spinning into the pit of despair and self-pity, I am as lost as I have ever been. What am I to do? I have no home or family now. I may go to another city to seek work but everyone knows travel for women alone is treacherous. The stories are plentiful of women who have tried to find extended kin on the road between York and Somerset.

The red-wigged angels begin to sing again to the glory of God. More forcefully this time. The tone of the audience has changed, and not because of the performers. At the start of a new scene, someone in black removes the arch and the stage is plain. As the actors reach the second measure of a song another sound can be heard coming from somewhere off stage.

"CLUCK CLUCK!"

I cannot help but laugh and shake my head. I hear the clucking again as if a chicken were trying to sing along with the players. Though she is shorter than most of the those that surround her, I finally spot Isca standing towards the front of the stage trying to accompany the performers above her. People are beginning to lose whatever small wick of patience they possess. I step toward the area of the stage and barely miss a puddle of dank water at the edge of the market.

To their credit, the angels have not stopped their

singing through the disruption, even when the skies get dark and a soft drizzle forms. They seem as though they've even begun to sing more fully, using gestures with their arms spread wide to further engage the audience. Isca begins to sing a little louder, and people start to yell directly at her. I move quickly into the melee of parcels, brown coats, gray hats, and the skirts of the few women.

I move Isca away with a gentle tug on her forearm and she yells, "Gads!" before she realizes it's me. A bruised and moldy tomato hits her squarely on the back of the head and it gives her the boost she needs to move away from the quadrant of townsfolk. She smiles. "I have met your boy twin, young lady."

Isca puts her face close to mine. We gaze at each other for a moment. Her stays are laced correctly. Her dark blonde braids are free of grass and straw and are neatly plaited. I can tell she has scrubbed herself clean. She looks overall more kempt in her appearance than when I saw her last. Except for the tomato remnants.

Isca insists that I join her at her home. At first I protest, but I am grateful and whisper through a tight throat, "Let us away then." We step together arm in arm, and then I succumb to a tearful spoken gratitude when she purchases little pies that have sweetmeats piping hot inside.

We leave the city for the small town of Holtswater. It is a long walk, but the weather holds and we keep company alongside each other. A sweet company indeed. We sing her little song on the way. *All is well and shall be well and well enough again.*

At this time of day, the small streets, lanes compared to the breadth of Exeter where coaches and carts can fill the width of roads, are noisy and crowded, tall horses with carriages and carts thunder by us. We walk quickly in the village and finally reach her home that is the upstairs flat of an old Tudor house near the south end of town. The stairs are small, and the steps feel uneven. At the top of the landing, I hear a man's voice humming softly. Isca opens the door. The apartment holds only three small rooms all with dark wood panels and very little sunlight. Half of the front room juts out over the narrow stone road.

The day's drizzle has turned to rain. Isca moves the iron bar and opens the thick wooden boards of the wide shutters just enough to let the air through. The tiny breeze cools the warmth from the back of my neck. We build up the fire together and dry our shoes. I lay my monk's cloak half-folded beside it. But I stay near the fire. The first warmth I have felt in days.

Isca introduces me to Hamlyn who knew me once as Matthew. He smiles as soon as he sees me, costumes be damned. He touches my forearm and then looks at me with concern. "Mathilde, it is good to see you again. If the stories are true, I am sorry for thy pain." He tells me I am welcome to stay. I begin to weep. He pats my shoulder and we stand together for a time.

Isca goes to another part of the house and quickly returns with a dull white chemise and long gray tunic along with a wide belt. No shoes to speak of, but thankfully she brings a pair of hose in decent condition.

"A proper milk maid!" Isca is proud of her work,

having dressed me as one would a favorite poppet. She fastens the silver buckle and stays of the belt, but she has trouble cinching up the sides of my skirts with pins. I finish for her and push my sleeves up above my elbows, then hold out my hands. Her eyes grow big with another idea. "Oooh, you can come and work with me at the dairy!"

I make a home in their small abode. Most nights, we eat salted whey and sip broth at a table pushed near to the hearth to stay warm.

Isca finds every opportunity to discuss fairy events. She seems to draw many of her decisions based on how fairy folk might respond. She will not go near the woods outside the village gate at night because the trooping fairies would not approve. Or worse, they might lure her into the otherworld for one thousand years.

One night at dinner, Isca says, "Everyone knows that the fairies cure and cause most diseases. They know about herbs and plants and the minerals and all the planets and can use them all together for their own will."

I say, before I can stop myself, "Do the fairies believe in helping those who have been victims of injustice?" Her eyes go wide.

But before she can reply, Hamlyn shakes his head and says, "It won't be a good idea to enlist the help of fairies. That is something that the church would disapprove of. Isn't this so, Isca?" She looks from me to her uncle and sighs.

I feel at ease with the uncle and his niece. They understand my story, and they are sympathetic, though for all of us life must go on and that includes my own life as well.

I harbor a fury I've never known before. About my stolen poetry, and the recent exposure of my womanhood. I no longer blame Saul but I do wish to find justice on my own on behalf of the liar who wears priest's clothes. How can I find peace unless he is dead or suffering?

I think about the brown leaf mask.

When the day arrives that I am introduced to the dairy owner, I brighten my smile and curtsy. He wears a wide hat and has a good humor. He tells me as long as I am producing milk from a cow to bottle and sell, and never steal from him, I can continue until at least the end of the season. I promise him these things. He looks me up and down and says, "I will pay ye to partner with Isca in her daily works. See if you can help retrieve some of the bottles that are unaccounted for."

I watch as Isca pulls the wide leather strap around her shoulders and affixes either end to a wooden crate that has twelve bottles of different size and material wedged within their compartments. Some are brown tin and tall, some are wider alabaster jugs and two are fancy glassware which look like they must be from Roman times. All the bottles are sealed at the top with wax and carry the mark of the dairy from which they were produced.

I look at Isca who beams at me proudly. I haven't noticed until now the strength in her arms, the wide measure of her shoulders. There is no way I could carry such a thing about town for a day. Nor would I want to.

Never forget who you are, Matty. Even when you must pretend.

Isca seems happy enough and I smile at her, pretending to enjoy the work but also grateful for her company and her generosity of spirit. From the new employment I will have money, though it is a pittance, and can contribute regularly to Hamlyn's hearth. But I hope to keep a pence or two for myself, so that I will make for myself a different future.

The house on Steepcote Hill is brick and half-timbered with its cobblestone street that meanders into a very shadowy lane. The wood, once whitewashed, is now blackened by soot and the elements. By the time we crest the hill carrying our small crate of bottles, Isca is trembling. We both wear shawls and though the day is mild, Isca sets her crate down and ties the shawl more tightly around her shoulders. She stops before we can knock on the green door, frozen. A white cat has come to see us, and its tail lifts, inviting us to pet it.

"That's her," Isca whispers.

"Who is 'her'?"

61

"The cat. The cat is Bessie Dunlop." Isca sets the crate down and moves away from the cat. It finds my skirts and makes its way behind me to brush up against my calf. I bend to scratch behind its ears. Isca wants to leave the bottles and go. I remind her we need to take the old bottles back to the dairy house.

I step to the door. Isca shouts, "No!" and begins to take the bottles out of the crate. A moment later, the door opens slowly with a creak. An old woman with a black shawl stands in the entrance. She has woolen stockings that rise just below her knees. I can hear a goat bleating from somewhere behind her. Her hand is at her heart, but then she lowers it and shakes her head, recognizing Isca. "Dairy girl." The old woman barks a laugh. There is a strangeness to the woman, but I don't think she is fairy. Though, how would I know?

Isca speaks to me from the side of her mouth. "You see? The cat is gone." Sure enough, the cat is nowhere. I resist mentioning that the cat could have been startled by Isca's cry.

"Young Isca, are you here to take my bottle away?" She laughs and spits. I can smell the smoke from the hearth in her kerchief as she asks us inside. She starts to say something, and then, covering her mouth, she tells us to wait at the door. Minutes later, she returns, relieved. "It would be far worse to break a bond with my friend Tom Leaf than to leave you wanting your milk jug forever more."

Isca is still, but I am curious.

"I asked Tom Leaf if I could discuss him with you,

and at first, he declined, but when I told him you were the rightful owner of his home, he obliged." She chuckles as if a small child has caused her to laugh. "Though he was begrudging all right. The scoundrel."

I can barely understand what she is referring to. Isca is rapt. Bessie nods and says, "You see, Tom Leaf has been living in my milk bottle all this winter now."

Isca shoots a look at me so quickly her little white cap comes loose. Bessie invites us into her house. At the back of the front room, at the hearth, lying on its side, is one of the dairy house milk bottles. It has two small cows etched into glass. Probably one of the diary's finer vessels. Isca sits down and studies the bottle. Inside it has a soft bed of moss and some dried berries. Fascination has overcome fear.

Mistress Dunlop puts us to work, spinning flax and milking goats. I don't know why she would have done otherwise since we showed up at midday. Any woman's work is full all day long. She should well know we will be missed at the dairy house and must return to our own multitude of tasks at home. That is when Bessie tells us how she sorely misses her grown son, whom she hasn't seen for over two years. She's convinced the boy she raised is a changeling swapped when he was a babe. He has always been one to wander off. That's why she has been courting the fairy Tom to help her.

Bessie's husband comes in, having clearly heard his wife talking. "God's nails, woman. You cannot continue this talk. You are no magic practitioner, and you're certainly no witch. Or are you?"

Isca is trembling. I stand, and we start to go. The husband pounds the wall next to the chair where his wife has a basket of peas in her lap. The peas spill onto her chair and roll to the floor.

Bessie hangs her head and weeps. In the smallest voice she says, "I want my son back."

"Petitioning the devil for help is not going to return a son to his mother." He storms out of the room. A picture on the wall tips to the left.

We bring five of the six empty bottles back to the dairy house. We tell the owner that one of the bottles was broken which is why there are five and not six. An older woman in dairy garb is brushing down the cows in their stalls, ropes from their harness tethered to the walls. One cow turns and gazes at me with large brown eyes as she chews her dinner.

I find milking a cow somewhat tiring and mostly mindless, although I jump and laugh when the hot spray of liquid hits the empty tin bucket the first time. After I become accustomed to the work, I create rhythms by the sounds of the squirt. The tin and the hiss combine to make a strange tone like that of a piper's call. Sometimes, I imagine the hot spray is so strong it injures Brother Andrew's left eye. At times, when I am starving, I squeeze the teat into my cupped hand and drink. I know it is frowned upon, but I have not been caught yet.

I don't see much of the other milk maids who work there. They are polite but distant. I observe the old and the young women who come through the doors at various times of the day to milk the cows or cap and deliver the bottles to families up the winding streets behind us. They titter at Isca's behaviors and give her a wide berth. There is a boy who comes and works the hay in the loft above us which also is the cheese loft. He is playful with Isca and waits until she is underneath the hole in the floor and then he dumps straw on her head, a yellow rainstorm meant only for her. At first, she laughs a little too loudly and I wonder if she enjoys the interlude to an otherwise tedious day. But she also grumbles afterward that the hay makes her itch.

On a day when the sun through the dairy house window warms the hay and raises the dank odor of the cows, I nod to three women who are bottling milk jugs. Isca wanders in behind me, and almost at once she is calling to all of us to see what she has found. Two mice, playing a strange little game. She offers to show me what they are doing by trying to jump on my back. I continue trying keep my voice calm, saying, "No, I am not interested in those games right now." The other women titter. They leave soon after, no longer concealing their laughter. Isca seems truly unable to comprehend what made the milk maids react in such a way when she tried to demonstrate, as she calls it, to "do as the mice do."

Normally, having to share Isca's small mat on the floor to sleep is not a bother. She has the fortune of owning more than one blanket, though the extra one

65

barely counts, being a threadbare quilt that she has had since childhood. By the time the daylight hours have simmered into twilight, I can no longer keep my eyes open, so I am rarely aware of her tumultuous turning as she makes herself comfortable. Sometimes Isca gazes into nothingness for long moments at a time. I wonder first what she may be looking at. After spending these many hours with her, I've observed this gazing is a part of her life. Her daydreaming life.

Isca bathes often, and her kirtle is clean. She has a second one for church, although from what I hear, she has been fined for her absence more than once. The young priest of the Holtswater parish has come round to Hamlyn's house twice sharing concerns not just about Isca's absences, but also about her thievery. I couldn't help but overhear the conversation Hamlyn and Father Salvi have about her taking communion wafers and bottling holy water.

After he leaves, Hamlyn begins to search through Isca's things. She arrives home from errands just as he opens the small set of drawers and pulls out the small white discs.

"Hey! Gads, Uncle! That is mine. I have taken it for better use!"

Hamlyn is clearly bewildered, shaking his head as he answers her indignancies. "It's an offense to your church and to God to be taking the body of Christ when it doesn't belong to you."

"I thought it belonged to everyone to make everything good again."

"It does, but you can't be the one helping yourself to it. You've already been fined for not going to services. Isca, don't bring trouble to our house."

"I use it to make goodness." She casts her eyes to her scuffed black shoes. She gives me a glance to see if I will turn this into a titter with her. I will not. Hamlyn makes mention of a cold hearth and socks that need darning, but Isca leaves the room as an answer. He glances at me, and I see in his eyes that I, too, am lacking in my contributions related to domestic chores. I never learned needlepoint or embroidery and we are far from woods where I know to hunt for foodstuffs. But I know where the town water well is and so I take two buckets and leave, one to start supper in the pot and another for cleaning.

When I return, there's only silence as Isca and her uncle rearrange the chairs in front of the hearth and open the windows. Even though the cold burns through the shutters, the sun still lingers in the sky a little longer and slips sidelong shafts of light across the window ledge.

Hamlyn turns to me with a solemn glance while we are sitting near the hearth. "Tonight there comes those that have traveled from parts near and far. There will be much in the way of deliberations that would be considered unlawful."

I tell him I am no stranger to deviance and that all confidences will be kept safe by me. Hamlyn grunts an assent.

When dusk arrives, and the sky turns to a painting of gray smoke with purple streaks, those invited crowd around the hearth, a small circle of near to twenty men pressed together with a few chairs and one small rug. I am soothed by this company somehow. I try not to stare, but I cannot help but admire the casualness of close elbows among the young and old. The soft tones they use, they know each other well. The men politely inquire to one another about family and the upcoming sowing season. Which farm animals are near to birthing. Who is of marriageable age. I perspire, the room is warm. Hamlyn introduces me as a cousin just arrived looking for work.

I can't see well because of the dim light and realize that this is purposeful; it shouldn't be evident who is here from anyone from the outside looking in. I must squeeze my eyes to focus. Two candles are lit and placed on the mantle. The fire is kept just high enough to keep the cold of the coming night away. Someone stirs the embers. And then walks through the door a man with green eyes whom everyone calls Jack Straw. I try to stop looking at him, but his eyes arrest my senses. I help Isca serve chunks of bread. I meander through the group, filling cups with a large pitcher. My skirts brush the edge of Jack Straw's coat. It is as if my clothing has caught fire.

I feel the heat all the way to my ears. I catch his eye briefly, and then he glances at Hamlyn, who says to all of us, "The new laws appear to affect rents in Exeter and the villages nearby."

I look to Hamlyn, unsure of what they are talking about. He says, leaning back in his chair, "Freemen and cottagers are more and more cast from their homes for lack of coin."

A man with a gray beard who looks to be about forty

years says, "The Vagrancy Act is also to be enforced."

He is referring to people without a home. I have heard neighbors talking about the beautiful cities of Venice and Paris, where hundreds of families are now homeless. According to the gossip, those that are without homes are called vagabonds. If arrested, they may be forced to work and fed only bread and water.

A young man wearing a brown coat that is too big for him speaks up. "Those that enforce the laws must be expecting a revolt."

"They are always expecting a revolt."

"Why call this meeting if not to act?"

Silence permeates the air. There is a clink of cutlery from the back room. Isca is either eating or preparing libations to share.

The man of about forty years who Hamlyn calls Kurt says, "We must do something. No more common land to hunt? The baron is out of his mind."

Jack Straw leans forward. There is a pock mark on his cheek. "This is no local lord. It is not just the nobility, but the church too. They will buy and buy again until they own more land than any duke or even the king." I am flummoxed by this man's presence. Oh, how the dance of his gaze anywhere near my direction stirs an ache low in my belly. And it's not just from the depth of his voice that echoes in my chest. Like a song written at the bottom of the ocean. Some look at him with trust, but I can tell that many do not know him. They are wondering, as I am wondering, how does he know what he purports to know? The mystery of him adds to the simmering flame.

Isca beckons to me and together we bring out the pitchers and refill cups. I sip from my own cup. The taste of cider is sour and crisp. I realize the wooden cup I drink from is cracked and move to pour the rest out in the basin before it drips all over my skirts.

Hamlyn sits back in his chair and sips from his cup. "Friends, we must abstain from feeding our fears and grow instead an agreement of what we want. We have strength in numbers."

Kurt says, "It was near three months ago, a group of men calling themselves Servants of the Fairy Queen broke into the Duke of Buckingham's Park while he was off giving a royal address. They helped themselves to a deer hunt."

The young man in the coat says softly, "Maybe action in stealth is the way. Sneak into the castle at Ludlow where King Arthur abides –."

Hamlyn speaks. "No. It would be foolish. The entire country is preoccupied with the health of the Princess of Wales. Every guard is on alert."

"Are we all to be vagabonds? To live and starve while others rejoice in their wealth?"

"Even in the days of our grandfathers, when the worker owed his lord, there was always food left. There was always the commons."

When Jack speaks again, I cannot help but notice how tender his voice is. "There is a world of difference in what the wealthy see and how we live."

What wisdom is this that pours from the mouth of he who has captured my attention, unlike anything I've ever felt? How soft and sure his tone as if in some other life he was a hero such as one of those told to me by the sisters of Blessed Comfort. Is Jack Straw a young Odysseus clothed in drab garments as if to hide his true lineage? Does the man have some kinship to great warriors who fought not for glory but to set things right?

And then he says, "The poor become poorer."

Hamlyn leans in, but I notice he has not committed to any actions that are being suggested by these brothers-in-whispers. "Aye. Jack Straw, what is the state of your camp?"

There is quiet. The fire hisses from a wet log. Then the green-eyed man says, "My encampment has over one hundred men, and they will make their demands anon."

The bearded man asks, "Which are…?"

"There are twenty-nine demands."

"You will need more men."

The man in the coat interrupts, saying, "I was told the city of Somerset offers good wages to men of twenty years."

Jack adds softly, "Every poor soul who is not of the royal court will soon be driven to the cities, and any money earned will be spent on the rents."

I ask, "Who will tend the abandoned fields?"

Everyone grows quiet; then Hamlyn shakes his head. "Everyone I know in the hill towns is replacing seeds with sheep."

"Giving away the commonlands to sheep?" Someone near the window is spitting the words. I can catch new errant discussions starting around me. They say that sheep's wool is the new economy, at least for those who are landowners.

Before Hamlyn can comment, Kurt says, "Plenty of ways to show the authorities our disdain for the state of things." Everyone looks at him. "Have you heard of the rogue mistresses of the night? They are a force that few expected."

There is a sullied tone to his voice. "Crones most of them. Pack of foolish women."

Jack Straw says, "They are all that has stopped the progress of the enclosures north of here, at least somewhat."

Someone quickly adds, "For now."

People begin to talk amongst themselves. By the tone, the rogue mistresses have now become legend. There is laughter and jollity at the mention of their larks. These women pulled up fences from newly bought lands by the church on the eve of March the first, leaving the ditches filled with only muddy banks.

Men begin to break into smaller groups.

Does love begin with a glance? I think it does. The last to go is the man with green eyes, who arrests my senses. I study him unashamedly when he has his back to me, appraising his dark brown hair and wide shoulders. He almost knocks over the chair but quickly grabs the back of it as it tilts sideways. I am tilting sideways.

He leaves then, nodding to Hamlyn and smiling at Isca who gives him a wave. Before he crosses the threshold into the dark stairwell, he looks over his shoulder and nods at me with a bare hint of a smile. I watch him go.

I can't tell if it's because of my stare or not, but Hamlyn

says, "You be careful. That one is a horse thief."

I go to town with Hamlyn, carrying some empty milk bottles on my lap. When he isn't terribly occupied with deliveries, he helps Isca and me to collect bottles or deliver milk that's further away. We talk about getting a second cart, but it's already costly keeping one nag and the cart down the road from the house.

On a day that was sure to promise snow, the cold reaching my bones that reminds me of my time at the monastery, we set off from the dairy.

My deliveries are near the marshes by the river. Hamlyn says he has business near there and so we set out along the open fields near the hollow buildings, old warehouses empty since the plagues were at their worst. There's word they will rebuild here soon. Crows gather near the water. They call to each other, and one flies off with food in its mouth. A second crow follows it. I wonder if they share with each other.

The fields are fallow, brown dead grass smooths the way as if great boulders have flattened the stalks. As we get near the wet road at the bottom of the hill near the river, which is high. Ice caps float along next to us as the waters stretche along us as we ride. Waterfowl are fewer today. Usually, in the spring one can spot swan or geese. The cold keeps us all shivering in our nests.

We arrive at one of my deliveries, a new one, and I see

the boy who was at Hamlyn's meeting, a boy who in the daylight looks younger than I thought. I knock at the door and place the bottles on the stone before the step.

I go to look for Hamlyn and see the boy again. He sees me but it is obvious he has work to attend to. Instead of the overly large coat, he now has on a proper wool tunic that carries a sigil for the manor house down the lane from the barn. Hamlyn leans over and tells me, that's Nicklas.

Inside a fence behind a set of stables is a field where eight horses that were grazing a moment ago in a cluster now move apart and wander further away from the barn.

It starts to snow.

The boy trudges further out into the field. He has a rope in his hands. He's approaching the largest one. I look to the entrance of the stables and see Jack Straw standing not ten steps away from me, watching the boy.

Nicklas holds the rope in front of him. I can hear him making soft noises. One of the geldings is neatly shorn but wears a blanket, and the others have thick winter fur. Especially a tall black horse. I see no markings on it. He is the largest in the field, easily eighteen hands tall.

The boy must go deep into the field to catch it. The snow turns to large floating flakes.

When I come back, I stand with Hamlyn. The wind begins to blow. Makes my wet skin even more uncomfortable, my fingers burn with cold. Nicklas has put the rope around the gelding with the blanket and begins to lead it into the barn. Hamlyn and I go to stand under the eaves of the barn to watch.

The horse being led by the rope starts to resist. Nicklas

lets go, and a distant horse, the largest in the field, begins a full gallop straight towards him. He stands frozen but then begins to move out of the way, thinking maybe the horse will run straight to the barn. The horse swerves towards its moving target.

The sound of hooves comes closer fast. The horse is headed straight for Nicklas. He is charging Nicklas.

Jack Straw moves quickly through the fencing and reaches the field. He calls out to the boy from twenty feet away. "Stand perfectly still." We can just barely hear him over the wind.

"I can't!"

"I mean it."

Nicklas doesn't move. Jack moves slowly towards Nicklas and the charging horse. The sound of hooves pounding gets louder. Hamlyn says a little prayer. Jack reaches the boy, and just as the thundering devil comes within three feet of them, Jack moves in front of Nicklas and stares directly at the beast, his hands out in front of him, as if to say, *Is this what you want?* The horse veers off in a different direction at the last possible minute.

Nicklas visibly exhales, so very relieved. Jack Straw makes the sound of a nicker with just enough noise so the horses come toward the barn. Even the ill-mannered horse follows. Routine takes over; Nicklas and Jack hang up ropes, unclasp halters, fill oat buckets.

Hamlyn and I join Nicklas and Jack at a little thatched roof house near the barn. We drink steaming tea from wooden bowls while Jack Straw stokes the fire in the hearth. We pull our chairs closer and listen to the snow turning to sleet against the windows.

The same wide dark coat and length of hair falls to his shoulders as the night I first met him. Does he remember me?

Nicklas is staring at nothing. After a while, he wipes his face with his sleeve. "He's a demon."

"He'll be put in the pen for it," Jack replies.

"It was a miracle."

Jack gives the younger a plain look. "No, it wasn't. It was knowing the ways of the horse." We sit quiet and drink our tea. His eyes find mine.

I ask, "How long have you lived here?"

Nicklas laughs, a small child's giggle. "He don't live here; he's a wandering dog. He lives everywhere. *I* live here." Jack smiles and shrugs.

Hamlyn and I give our thanks and stand to leave. The snow is now coming in thick and heavy. Jack says he has business in the city, and Hamlyn offers him a ride. By the time we get to the road, the snow has coated most everything, all brown field and cobble lane blanketed in winter's whiter rest.

Back in Exeter, I turn to the crowds drifting near and around me. Everyone hurries along, hands in muffs and heads in hoods. The wind at our backs keeps us from getting too comfortable. Everyone wears a gaze of being warmed by the fire. The cold pushes against my headscarf.

We end up walking the cart and horseback to the top of high street. On a sunny day we would be standing in the cathedral's shadow but for now its white stone towers defy the clouds behind it.

As Hamlyn cleans snow and mud out of Sheba's shoes, I turn to Jack but just as I open my mouth to speak, the wide clang of bells rings out for the little nine o'clock eucharist before the daily mass. Jack Straw startles at the sound and then we both laugh at this coincidence. The ringing comes to its end.

"Perhaps next time, I will startle you with my poems instead of bells."

"Is that how you would prefer it my lady?" He does not stop smiling. Therefore, I cannot either.

Later the next day, the snow has stopped but the cold is unrelenting. After spending hours pulling on pink udders for untold moments, I stop. My hands have cramped. I lean my head on Ruthie's belly, an eight-year-old heifer. I stroke her fur. She is full of warmth and gentleness. She has dark brown eyes and a tail that moves fast enough to split an egg.

I have gone somewhat into a dull trance as I sit on the milking stool, rubbing my hands and petting Ruthie's fur. I think about the sensation of the warmth of the late day sun on my face, hoping for an early spring. I don't notice that anyone has entered. I am about to drink the warm, almost clear liquid I've just squirted into my hand when I'm startled by a man's voice. I wipe the milk away on my skirt. He is standing close to me, in shadow. He smells like leather and the wild scent of brambles before they bloom.

"I have caught sight of the deity who wears the moon on her brow. Come down, maid of heaven, and alight the senses of my heart."

I almost squirt milk in his face, so completely taken aback am I by his words. I have never heard a man speak that way, much less to me. I pretend to be unimpressed. The greenest eyes stare down at me—full of mirth and a touch of mischievousness. We laugh. He has remembered our last meeting.

He asks if he may join me as I work and helps to bottle some of the heated milk, a process that is important in keeping the milk safe to drink, from the buckets retrieved from a stove next door. There are streaks of hot liquid running along our fingers. He tells me he has heard that I know how to compose words. He says he can tell by the way I talk. I shrug.

I tell him how I once planned to be a writer like some of the famous women of the court or of the clergy. I tell him how my little book of verses was taken from me by a friar I once trusted.

He asks gently, "How does a poetess end up in a cowhouse?"

"I am not who I once intended to be."

"None of us are," he says. His eyes are soft, tender. I feel a rush of emotion.

After a minute, I say, "What do you want?"

He doesn't answer; he just watches me work. I grow uncomfortable with this and turn my back to him. Two other milk maids come in and draw Jack's attention away. I pretend not to care.

He leaves and returns the next day. He buys four bottles of milk and departs again.

The following day, he does not visit and I wonder what has come of it.

As the snow begins to melt and what is left grows thick with mud and sewage that borders each of the little streets, he comes more often. Some of our conversations are frivolous, some more private. He tells me about his mother and his aunts, who were condemned for witchcraft when he was a boy. He tells me that they were all healers. His mother was also considered one of the wealthiest widows in the west country at the time. He tells me with closed eyes that she went to church every week and used her ointments only for goodness. Jack talks to me so quietly that I am brought to tears by the pain that sits at the edge of his words.

After sitting in silence for a while, he says, "I have not once doubted the need to become who I am in order to live in a fairer world." His eyes glow as he comes up with a new idea. "Come see the rebel camp. There are women that are a part of our cause. We are not the scoundrels you think we are."

Isca appears more and more defiant of the church and her uncle's wishes. She says that Bessie Dunlop's son returned home after two years away. He had been a participant fighting on behalf of the Commonwealth and was injured in one of the altercations on Mousehole Heath. He suffered a broken foot and hobbled home on a Sunday in time for dinner. Isca adds, "I suppose sooner or later, Bessie Dunlop must give us back our milk bottle."

On the way home from the dairy, she takes a stick and draws a circle around us in the dirt. I don't know what to make of it. She takes from her apron pocket a small communion wafer and sets it in the middle of our circle.

"What would you ask of the fairies?" Who is this woman who, days earlier, didn't know how animals reproduce?

My voice is low and unhesitant. "Where is my book, the one I wrote those many months ago?"

She nods and pours a little water from a flask in her hand and spits into her palm, swirling the liquid around, then ceremoniously pours it on the wafer.

"It is under the bed."

"It's not under the bed!"

She's already walking ahead. "I didn't say it was under your bed." She stops and looks down at her hand. She watches me for a moment. "Bessie Dunlop asks why you haven't come with me to visit her. I told her it was because of a boy and Bessie said to me, 'It will take a long time to truly know what's in his heart."' A pause then. I believe there is truth in her words.

Isca leans in so that our heads are almost touching. "Where do your words come from, Tildee?"

"Wouldn't everyone argue everything comes from God?"

She and I look at one another. The silence tells all; we both believe that it's not such a simple explanation. I say, "From the birdsong, from the daybreak." I am reminded of the first time I had use of writing instruments at the abbey; a basket of quills, a knife to sharpen the points. How I once complained about finger stains, which I now think of as a gift from all ink pots. I stare down at my hands. Dry as husks and ruddy red but otherwise stripped of blue-black smears.

I tell her it started with a dream.

OAK HILL, LONG AGO

My earliest memories include a yellow straw-thatched roof and a sandy cove. Inside there was a tiny stool where I sat weaving horsehair and course twine for Mother to use in her work. My parents were common folk fashioning nature's gifts as tools and charms. My father fought in two revolts, then perished in the third. Twice he tried to teach me to defend myself and twice I disappointed him. I am clumsy whenever I pick up a knife or sword.

My mother kept alive words that spoke about the women in our family who lived before the plague, before the monasteries were built in valleys of the east and atop the hills in the west. After my father died, I followed my mother around all the many hours while she hunted for morels or left offerings to the fairies at the base of trees or in the branches.

She often referred to a power that was greater than a mallet or an ax. She said we learn it with prayers and ceremony such as those led at festivals in the hills on the Solstice plains. Before one of the festivals of midsummer when I was near to eight years old, she gave me a gift of a small figurine shaped vaguely like a woman's body made of dark polished stone and smoothed over time to fit perfectly in the palm of one's hand. She said it carried the spirit of those who lived in a time long ago when the earth and heavens were one. A mother's allocation of power to her daughter. She called it her Thumbelina, a charm that she claims kept her alive while she gave birth to me.

But even though the trees gave her solace and the rocks sang her stories, nothing could cure her of the sweating sickness. No blessed lady came to save her. Before she died, she made sure I found somewhere to live with the sisters of Cornwall Abby. For years she had gathered and harvested elderberry for use in a health tonic for the sisters of the convent. But during the first summer after Mother passed, Nettie and Brother Samuel said I could stay on the floor near the hearth in the back room of Odebury's church.

I think I lived in the woods more than anywhere else that summer. I felt a closeness with everything that ran, hopped, slithered, and flew so I learned to never feel alone. To me, divinity lived in the tree roots, salvation in the moss, company was the shadow on the hillside.

We could hear his coughing before catching sight of him on the southern hill of Odebury's parish foraging for asparagus, a peculiar plant stalk cultivated in France but now grows wildly in England. Samuel is not her husband. There was a time when he wanted to leave the church so they may be together but Nettie convinced him that I was not worried for my soul. There were times when she thought I wasn't listening. She and Samuel whispered in the dark.

"As long as I do not get with child, people will mostly ignore our union. As long as we are discreet."

I helped Samuel pick the asparagus spears which I placed in my wide basket until a coughing fit sent him doubled over. So painful to hear the endless rupturing of his chest. He sounds as though he might never stop.

"Come, I will heat you some broth."

I'm relieved to see him outside, but I knew it was only pretend for the people who call him Brother Samuel. He went grudgingly back to his old cot in a room in the back of the church. Thankfully, the hearth was wide and the cot beside it so he could get as warm as possible without the showers of embers burning his thin wool blankets.

He tried to rally his spirits on my behalf because the pain in my eyes was a mirror revealing the truth of all things. He sat up and coughed. Waved it away as though it were nothing, though I saw the bloody spittle that he wiped from his palms.

Nettie returned from her rounds, tending to those ill and in need. New mothers, older mothers. Women whose knuckles can't bend anymore.

"I have a gift for you," he says, trying to rally. He ruffles through a satchel next to the bed and pulls out a printed herbal. "*Tractatus Herbarum*, and newly translated to the common tongue! A scribe from Exeter has just delivered it."

"Samuel, even translated it will not suit me. I am not book learned like you." She turned her face away.

"I will read you the entire book in my liturgical voice." He coughed a little, pretending it was part of the performance.

"Mint, marjoram, peony, and pennyroyal…wonderful for the womb…" he looked to her, eyebrows raised. She smiled at him and I could see the girl in Nettie just barely. In her small laugh, there was young love that seeped beyond her gray hairline, beyond the lines framing her eyes. "Oh, but you already know all this, don't you, Milady?"

She shrugged. He continued, "Then, how about this part:'Rue, when soaked in wine and myrrh, can cause the flow.'"

I had no idea what he was talking about, especially when it came to plants, but I knew it was part of their closeness. Brother Samuel and Nettie Dedham spent many hours of the day experimenting with new plants. I usually followed behind, trying to listen, trying to be good.

Every so often I was allowed to put little plants with thriving roots into the soil next to the church and hope they would grow. I checked on my most recent plant bed. The one with the tiny fragile leaves had taken root. Its bluish clusters carry an odd scent and, with it, stories of medicine from old wives' tales. I wished to know more from the plants that Nettie called *the sour herb of grace for women*.

She said, more to the book than to Samuel, "The author sounds a little like Hieronymus. Who can afford myrrh?"

Samuel provided Nettie with sources of information of the ancient and modern provisions of herbal lore. Alongside other books he'd brought her, Nettie appeared to take an interest in the official names of plants, like those with proper Latin titles, like *artemisia*, which grew wild on the edge of the woods. But whenever it was just Nettie and I herb foraging, she called the plant *mugwort*.

Some plants contain powerful remedies. I will never know if my mother knew about these medicines, but Nettie spent those years when she wasn't making rounds and catching babies, using all of her free hours to determine how plants worked. She told me she was always on the hunt to treat the mysterious illnesses that afflicted the womb.

She made everything seem like a simple process to cultivate the plant, mined from the soil, after being stripped and washed. Calling the leaf, the sap, or the flower – and of course the root, the home of all potency. A plant could speak to her in smell or taste, like a mourning dove that sits so still and quiet and then erupts into sudden flight. Such power of these herbs and plants could hold her for hours, tasting, boiling, chopping, spitting.

The continuous excavating of herbs and plants was often tedious to me. I must have been ten years old trying to recall the names of plants, always at Nettie's heels, following her through woods and meadows. Brother Samuel one night tested me on the name of a plant and when I could not identify it, he got a gleam in his eye.

One night before supper, he said to Nettie, who was deep in her thoughts, "Sing with me." She turned away from the black pot she was tending to, gave him a sour look and turned back to her broth.

"No."

"I want to hear your voice make sounds like the hum of a bee."

"I can't sing," she muttered.

"You could affix your own words to one of the hymns I know."

"I'll be strung up for it later."

"No, Nettie, my dove, let us sing this herbal in plainchant. Together."

"I shall sing to myself another time."

"By my hand, Nettie, you infuse God's love through the song, as your plant's medicine is infused in the tea." After a long moment of silence that felt like two years to me, she sighed.

"Very well." Then, "Don't laugh."

He sang some words of the plants he knew. This proved irresistible to Nettie, for nothing filled her heart with joy as did the talk of her medicines. After a bit, she grew more courageous and began to mumble the names of herbs and plants long etched upon her own heart: *Borage, Anise, Angelica, Lavender. Rue, Chamomile, Mint, Feverfew. Primrose...* She started to sing a variation of Samuel's song. I could see it in her eyes, that welled with tears, she would sing that song forever after for all of the important reasons of her life.

Sam laughed. She laughed. We laughed. A new plainchant was born that night. It was one of the last nights when Samuel was still strong and in good humor. This song remained with Nettie and I forever after. We began to practice the chant to call to mind the remedies in a melodic way that also honored Samuel's memory.

Weeks later, Brother Samuel was abed more than not. One day, I hopped up on the cot near the fire and put my head against his shoulder. I could feel a rumble like stones in his chest. I often prayed that the fairies would take away his pain. Sometimes, he told me that my prayers had worked. That day he did not.

He was very pale. His beard could not hide the gauntness of his jawline. Sometimes Nettie trimmed the edges below his chin. I would clean up the trimmings and his bedpan in a ditch outside behind the collapsed western wall.

He drank the broth I made hot for him pouring it

from a ladle into an old wooden bowl sprinkled with some dry onion. Nettie came in and sent me to gather little white and yellow flowers that smelled like honey found on the hillside. I shut the door to make a sound as though I was walking away but then tip-toed back toward the darkness of the room instead.

"Anything to bear me hence?" He says, trying to smile.

"Why would you joke?" She sat next to him, took the half empty bowl of broth away and held his hand.

"You could do it?"

"Do what? Say it."

"Send me through the dolmen door." They both began to weep in that moment. Nettie said, "I love you," but no other words would come out. After a minute, when the only sounds were the sounds of the fire in the hearth, they began to speak the reality of Brother Samuel's end. I could barely see them through the blindness of my weeping. Nettie caught me suddenly standing in the doorway.

I'm worried she will scold me, but instead, she wiped her eyes with her old, stained apron. "Ah, Mathilde, sweet cherub. Fetch us a large pitcher of water from the well for our dear friar." She thought I had already gone and returned. I placed the jug outside of the room. I stared at her, not understanding. Couldn't the fairies and their medicine heal him? Why would they lead Samuel through the dolmen door, which everyone knows means he would travel through a long night's procession to the otherworld?

And then came the day he said to me, "One day, Mathilde, the army of God will become like a tempest in their fight to overthrow the spirit of the wood, and I will not be here to hold back the rising tide." I was confused by his message, words shared in bare guttural utterances while he lay on his bed for a final rest. Nettie tried to usher me out of the room so she could bathe him and allow him his dignity.

The room stank of not just death that hovered nearby but by bodily waste and food soiled on his night shirt and on the bed. There seemed to be no air left in the room. Sometimes, Nettie and I wore cloth around our faces to protect our nostrils from the reek.

Nettie said to Samuel, "Speak not, beloved," but he ignored her and looked at me as plainly as he could.

He closed his eyes, and I was dismissed.

THE VISITATION, FAIRY REALM, OUT-SIDE OF TIME

He's dressed in fine robes, dark purple velvet and fur such as a prince might wear. I've never seen a color like it except for maybe a late day sky in April. His raiment is quite different than the impoverished dark brown wool and roping of his order. His beard is trimmed tight against his face. His eyes are laughing. His cheeks are plump, pink, full of life and laughter. He offers me his hand. Nettie joins us, and they embrace. Then Samuel offers Nettie his hand, and they circle in an ancient dance around the fern beside the wide sweep of may apple.

The woodland seems brighter than it was a moment ago. There is a hush around us, and a circle of light appears from deep within the din of the wood. So gold and bright it clinches at my heart. The radiance alights upon the turn of the leaves and the reach of the climbing vine. Twig and branch appear as if many tiny sparks have been sprinkled upon them. All grows quiet. The fairy pageant appears from the darkest part of the wood. First, there is the sound of laughter, like tiny bells. There are small children prancing upon the old path, knees raised high in a merry march. They carry high lanterns with long sticks made of blue bell flowers sprouting candlelight.

She comes, the Fairy Queen. Her dark gold tresses fall in waves reaching a waist cinched with a silver belt. Her green gown unfolds in a train, a cascade of rich fabric upon the ground behind her. Her gaze is winsome. There follows the rest of the procession behind her. Her gait sets the pace. Lords and ladies of untold years wear faded lace and their glance seems to see the invisible. They move as if they float. Clothing cannot contain the wide array of class; the colors are faded lilac hues. They are a pageantry of *otherfolk* that is endless. There is soft song. Not joyful or sad. More like a breath of the forest, a hum of creation. No break of leaf under foot, their graceful promenade are gentle footfalls upon the earth. And all of nature watches, listens.

Sam kisses Nettie's fingertips, and he turns to walk into the woods, joining the twilight procession. I wave farewell. The yearning in my heart is released by a thin sound, barely a cry. I am afraid to disrupt this marvel, this golden apparition. Samuel turns once more as he dissolves into the whole of the *otherfolk*, his purple clothing turning to lavender, spiraling into silver light, starlight. I call out to him one last time. I hear the whisper of his voice that echoes in the hollow of the trees. He seeks the isle of silver apples. Samuel gazes first to me and then to Nettie. He is gone.

If life is made of memories, then eternity is made of dreams. Suddenly, my spirit was infused with a wildness that united my heart and my head. My eyes were open. I was alive for the first time in my life.

A few weeks after Brother Samuel passed away, I went to live with the sisters of the Blessed Comfort. I began to collect water from St. Bridget's springs. The sisters of the abbey were grateful for the holy water that I brought to them. This act, I suppose, forged a foundry of trust. We used the water to heal burns and scrapes, to bless ourselves and be soothed in our corner of a frightening world.

They found my Thumbelina and crushed it with a hammer. When Nettie brought in sweet smelling herbs, the sisters forbade us to thank the fairies. They taught me to thank God for His medicine. I spoke my poems aloud only to the stream and wood, the rocky banks that bordered the meadow, to the passing faun. At the convent, I learned that everywhere was sacrifice. I learned my letters, but they were taught to become prayers. I breathed thought to words and words to sentences, but they became cloaked in the language of love. Every day since,

I have tried to capture the ecstasy of the gift of Samuel's departure.

Was it a dream, an enchantment? I will never be sure but it fed me sustenance for calling upon words to wrap like vines around a gesture of story, a tapestry of ideas. Little sentences I played with and as I grew into young womanhood the words coupled with thoughts of desire.

~ *There is no more perfect day then when one sits in the garden and everything has awakened. Can you hear the stirring in the tree roots, the tremble of many sounds below the rocks, inside the soil?*

~ *Does the green wood hold more spirit than the meadow? Can splendor coincide with worry and still be good?*

~ *Is this what rapture looks like? The moths that circle and feel along their way, a harmonic convergence of joy and desire?*

Brother Samuel's words of warning speak louder to me now than when he lived. I can hear his voice clearly, still. I know what he meant. It explains how I came to write about a love so true that reflected not the monastery's god but the spirit I kindle when I write, drawing from the essence of the deep wood and returning green.

ODEBURY, SEVERAL YEARS AGO

Nettie let me stay with her and help her with her duties

until she spoke to Lord Odebury on my behalf. To remain and to live to serve his lands. Mother Abbess spoke often about another grown mouth to feed in her nunnery. I learned quickly to grow and bundle the woad, a talent I discovered that came naturally. A plant of many uses, it grows wildly when cultivated and sometimes has two harvests in one season, but it can be hard to control. The seeds flourished when given rich, bone-heavy soil. Though it has medicinal uses, in Odebury, we cultivated woad for use as a special dye. Nettie showed me what woad could do; a plant soaked in rainwater and then with ash could magically transform linen and wool a soft, rapturous blue. I am proud to say the woad became a source of wealth for his Lordship of Odebury. This is how I secured my place at the nunnery for the years I lived at the Blessed Comfort.

Woad is used mainly for its dye properties, and it quickly became popular at the autumn faire. Everyone bought the large wax-capped jars of dark liquid from Oak Hill to Somerset. The Dorset guild became our biggest buyer. All official documents were happily approved and signed by Lord Eventide and the reeve, Paul Kent, who acts as both a protector and enforcer of the rules of Odebury. Kent helped us ensure the Odebury crest was affixed to our wares, which has provided a greater visibility to our manor.

When we began to grow more plants to sell small jars of her procured medicines I told Nettie she should sell her herbs to the cooks or physicians of London. Oh, even better, we should, under the pennant of Lord Odebury, travel north to beg an audience with nobles. But Nettie could not envision it. The ideas scared her. She accused me of loftiness and being childish for I was still a child. *Know your place.* She said this out of love and concern, but I did not understand.

NORTH EXETER WOODLANDS, TODAY

Jack and I join the group of camp men who cluster around small circles of low embers in the mist, where mud, horses, and carts are plentiful. We are fed camp cakes and turnips, and small apples from someone's cellar. Mine is bruised and mealy in parts, but probably the best I've ever had because it's placed in my hands by the green-eyed man. Perhaps it is my imagination, but when I bite into one, the flames of the fire, mostly gone to coals, leap up as if rekindled. I gaze at the sky and watch the clouds as they move quickly past. A cascade of stars emerges. It leads me towards thoughts of my immediate condition. I take a breath and exhale. My belly unclenches.

Some of the camp men begin to pack up their carts. They snuff lanterns and retire to lean-tos and small tents. They disappear into the yellow, foggy light. The clouds return.

I can't turn away from Jack Straw as I watch him make his rounds, checking on supplies, inquiring about recent wounds of man and horse alike. I imagine his stare making its way toward me. The color of his eyes is like the darkest stone at the bottom of the sea. His grin unsettles me, igniting a world of questions. His voice, low as the hum of a bee, is also like undisguised thunder, unnerving and exciting all at once. Though doubt lingers that the words will come, an urgency exists. I feel it ready to surface like the smell of spring after a lengthy winter burial. I plan to find a goose quill and ink. Yes – pouring thoughts onto paper feels like a doorway into newfound happiness.

But my thoughts are instantly upset as I see, in the clearing, a low cobbled fire that stokes below a large soup kettle. There sits a woman, huddled small, like an elf hiding in a barrow so different is she from the men who are meandering nearby.

Nettie.

I run to her and sob into her bosom. She strokes my short hair, revealed in all its continued horribleness.

I say to her as I wipe my eyes, "Aunt, I still look every bit a boy to anyone who knows me."

"Tsk tsk," Nettie Dedham answers, "True beauty shines through and through."

I hug her again. I smell the sprouted greens of Oak Hill at planting time. I stand, still unmoving, with my face in her braid.

Her hair is fully gray and wildly unkempt, her clothing worse. Even my cloak is not as mud-caked and horse-haired as her tattered shawl. When she stands and walks to gather her medicine bag, she teeters as if she is walking barefoot on thorns. But her gaze is direct. She looks me over, assessing whatever ills I have that might need tending to. I smile to assure her that I am faring well.

We talk through the late hours of the night. She tells me that the lord of the manor discharged her for the prestige of a physician who is university-trained.

Physicians now rival the number of midwives in this part of the kingdom. The final straw occurred when the church bought the land she had farmed and foraged her whole life – the common lands – acreage that had been in use for everyone since the Magna Carta. The Mother Abbess gave her a bed to sleep on the floor, but her bones ached so badly it drove her out.

The work in the camp has been consistent, she warrants, and she is paid for her expertise ministering to wounded men. That includes everything from infection to illness. No self-respecting university-trained physician would dare step foot into these woods, especially at night. She tells me she is knee-deep in her own mischief now that she is untethered to the manor and to Oak Hill.

I promise I will meet with her again soon.

THE DAIRY HOUSE

Jack returns almost daily to the dairy house. He isn't looking for milk, or other maids. Though we had formed what might be called a friendship, it is quite another thing to allow him a closer proximity to my body, to meet his glance without shutting my eyes tight or looking away, wretched as I still feel.

On a day that is brighter than the count of days since Candlemas, Jack tells me of the churchmen who have bought the lands north of Exeter. This includes lands where Nettie and folk from the manor had gone to hunt and to forage for many generations. I know these hallowed meadows, the woods where a moss-worn creek snaked through from one manor to the next.

And then he speaks the words that steal my breath. He tells me he has learned that the priest, Angelus Santos, has settled in a fine manor home on a large plot of newly bought land, and it is barely two leagues away. It is land enclosed by hedge and fence.

I feel a rush of sickness in my head, a roaring of blood coursing through what had once found stillness. It is as if some long incubating egg has begun to crack open. I rock forward and back. I ask him how he knows such a thing. Even though I told him about my stolen book, I never mentioned any names. I have only shared the name and the devilish action with one other person. Only Nettie knew the whole story. *Ahh. Of course.*

He says slowly, as if he is contemplating the possibilities, "There is logic in joining with me, for I can offer you coin from the very pockets of those who stole your life from you. He was your plagiarist, wasn't he?"

"What are you saying?" Although I know what he is saying, I want him to repeat the words.

"Think of it as retribution that God has not attended to as yet."

My brow furrows. "You would steal from a priest?"

"The church has stolen from my family." After growing quiet for a moment. "Their power knows no bounds. We must take what we can. When we can."

I dreamt about my mother last night. She died when I was eight. In waking hours, I never remember her voice or her embrace, but in my dreams I know her fully again. I know the tone of her simple chatter, the openness of her shoulders. In the dream, she is trying to warn me about the woods. All I see are fox pups playing on the hillside nearby. But when I turn to look for her, she is gone and the woods surround me. I hear an animal barking, like a fox – no, now like the howl of something more sinister, like a wolf who hasn't fed. I am afraid.

The next day, Jack brings me salve.

The jar smells like honey and beeswax. There's a flowery smell, too. Nettie would know which scents they are. Primrose? Calendula? He puts a tiny bit on his own fingertips and takes my hand while I pretend to occupy myself with cows.

He starts with my forefinger. Just the tip. Then the first and second knuckle. The touch of another human and the pull of his allure feels like a rush of a warm breeze in summer. Isca comes in the door at that moment and I pull my hand away, momentarily released from the enchantment. She makes a *tsk tsk* sound, giggles and leaves again.

Jack's gifts are instinctively those items I drastically need for my skin, luxuries I have no access to. He brings lavender and chamomile ointments for my hands, and then one day, he sits beside me and watches me work with Ruthie. I can tell with my back to him that he isn't observing my work but gazing at me, the whole of me. At one point, late in the afternoon, I notice that the warmth

98

of the sun fills the dairy, enhancing the scent of warm milk and hay. I stop what I am doing. He slowly, carefully, almost ceremoniously, takes the bonnet from my head.

I put my face down against the side of Ruthie's belly as I often do, and Jack reaches out to touch my hair. I know I can turn him away, and I fight within myself whether to let him go further. I weep because of how my scalp looks and feels; the hair has grown past my neck, dark stalks of unruly red tufts. There is also the problem with the lice.

He leads me to the back of the haystack underneath the windows where the sun is brightest. He has brought a small jar of pennyroyal oil this time. He rubs his hands together, and then he slowly and gently cinches his fingers through my tresses, several hairs at a time. He spends hours combing the lice and nits from each strand, and then he takes another jar of the lavender and peppermint crème, and he spreads it across my scalp, which feels cool and tingly.

"Where did you get the ointment?" Such a salve must be costly.

"Mistress Dedham gave it to me. Said you'd like it." I laugh out loud.

Before he leaves he washes and combs my hair again. He does not replace my kerchief. I weep in ecstasy at his touch. He does not grab my breast. He does not seduce me as if I must now repay a debt to his kindness.

The next time he comes to the dairy and when I am sure we are alone, I begin my life again.

I fall into his arms. It is a surrendered collapse. The weight of isolation, the cruelty of how cold my skin and bones have felt until now, drives me to him like a heavy rope. He kisses me everywhere he can, along my neck and arms. Tiny, gentle sweeps of his lips.

We find a private corner behind the haystacks. He lays his coat atop some loose straw. Always a possibility the owner will come any minute. Does that make my heartbeat faster knowing that we may be caught, or is it the feeling of rapture that resonates in my body that I have never answered to before? That until now I have only imagined.

HOLTSWATER

After a week of our courtship, I am sitting on a small, three-legged milking stool by the window in the dairy house, the smell of dung and straw buoyed by the sweetness of fresh milk. I am moving slower, not bound by finite rules. The weeks of playing dairy maid are dull, but there is an easiness in the pace of life that is an unexpected found kindness. The sunlight is at my shoulder, warm. My mind is free of care and worry, and I am aware of a quiet stillness.

A spark catches on the fabric of my heart. I think of Jack, and the words erupt quite on their own. "*Rapture, must I wait until I find thee? Would it be in mid-summer when the fruit is swollen? I imagine we are food for one another. Let us not starve for long.*"

I am eager to please another person. When Jack arrives we sup together, then begin to practice the faith of our passions almost every day. Whether the cows are watching or not.

When I return to Hamlyn's house every night and try to sleep, it is fitful, night after long night. Isca tells me it is as if she is lying next to a large rabbit caught in a trap. She says that I cry out. I feel a weight carried, too, through the day, but cannot pinpoint its source. After a week of this, she finally confides, "Tilda, I believe the fairies have cursed you." I ask why they would do such a thing. She shrugs. I dream of the book Brother Andrew stole. In the dream, he buries it under silt at the bottom of Mother Abbess's fishpond.

Isca has been composing as well. Sometimes, I catch her staring into nothing, curled up on the stuffed mattress beside the wall. Her knees are pressed to her chest. After days of seeing her do this, I realize that the compression is affecting her breathing. When she sings, her voice is lower than before, and the measure of the song is less plain, with more of a lower cadence. An utterance, more a peculiar dissonant melody. She begins to sing a little fairy song. *In times of barren land, come, Tom, come, Tom, we need your hand. Sheep and wool aren't enough for me. Come, Tom, come.*

There are more changes in Isca. Her popularity with neighbors and various townsfolk has grown. She is the milk maid who charms her customers and always has a quick response to add to the gossip of the day.

She says to Mistress Agnes Wagner on Church Hill Road, "I heard tell that Mrs. Wallace is readying to deliver her seventh babe. She who always dresses in a gown that has gold thread and a fur-lined collar."

Mistress Wagner's eyes grow round. "Aw, yes, paler than cream, that one. She's hid her belly well."

"No wonder, she is part of the wealthy family of landowners near to Cornwall. Probably living on clotted cream and scones all her life."

Isca looks to me and gestures as if to include me in the conversation. Nettie Dedham, up until recently, had always been their midwife.

Mistress Wagner has already moved on to the next tidbit of information. "I heard that her husband, Master Wallace, was accused of selling putrid meat from Oak Hill's market last week…"

Isca gasps, "He will be pilloried," and then her voice trills in enthusiasm, "And made to eat his own rotten meat!"

The woman, Agnes, says, "I knew a vintner who was forced to drink his own foul wine and whatever was left in the barrels was poured over his head."

"Not so rare a thing."

I pull Isca away from the town talk to continue our deliveries wondering if this is what I should be writing about. Stories instead of verses. Is this what is important to the common folk? I was bored by the women's talk but Isca is striding quickly with her braids tossed like a proud pony on a gusty day.

And in the days to come, I notice new things, costly

things, about the house. A new tablecloth, a new pewter cup, even a pretty shawl for Isca. Hamlyn asks her how she has acquired these things, and she shrugs with an offhanded reply, "I got these things fairly, they are gifts from the neighbors." Hamlyn and I look at each other blankly.

DEVON, IDES OF MARCH

The night is black as ink. A group of women, eight of us in all, are in the middle of a large field where, besides the occasional glimpse of a bounding hare or flit of a night bird, only the line of a fence can be seen by the lantern light. The camp men are nearby and wait at an owl's hoot of a distance, keeping a fire and hope for our safe return.

I'm told we're trespassing on Angelus Santos's newly bought home. When I mention this to the women next me, they shrug. They believe that no one resides in the old lofty manor on the other side of the hill because until recently it bore the mark of a red cross painted on the door.

The field is bare of early shoots. Except for maybe the spring onion which we can smell on the breeze. Otherwise, nothing has grown here for some time. There is green and brown patchwork on the land. I poke my small shovel into the earth and begin to dig. I find a stray shell amid the packed earth that cups rather well in the palm of my hand.

It is the fencing that is new.

We make barely a sound as we work. Dogs sound an alarm well to the east of us, and we glance at one another, hopeful that no master will rally on the hound's behalf. There is no moon because of the cloud cover, but we have our lanterns to stack atop one another on the back of the cart. Besides shovels, we have buckets of water to pour over the corner posts, which are hard to remove. Some of the roots of the hedges are even more deeply rooted. Some focus more on the base of the hedge, hacking at them as if a tree to cut down. Others use the shovels to pull the roots apart.

We are women of the region come to write our cause in the soil with shovels and rope. Nettie stands close enough to me so we can talk as we work. "Are you happy staying in Holtswater now, Matty girl?" She's got smears of mud on her face and arms. I look at both our feet and note that our shoes are not made for this kind of labor. I walk a little higher because of the layer of mud stuck to my soles. Our coats and shawls have been thrown on the back of the cart. Someone passes a jug of ale around. It's tart and strong, adding to the spark of the night.

I give a nod as an answer to Nettie, and my breath is a vapor riding on the air.

I glance behind me and see that our group is intermittently hidden by low white fog moving in from the hills in the distant west.

The earth yields itself in clumps but the going is long and tedious. I ask Nettie about her other excursions. She says, "Only been to one other. It rained that day, so some of the fencing pulled up easily. Twelve of us laboring like clawing rabbits searching for a new den." She laughs, then sits down for a bit.

One of the women, Aldamara, is about Nettie's age, taller than most men with hips as wide as the length of my arm. She is the cook of Odebury, a small manor east of Exeter. Aldy, as Nettie calls her, professes to not have an opinion of how low her skirts fall to cover her black stockings, which tonight fall just below the middle of her calf. Such disregard for propriety is met with her fellow cook, Nannie's, disapproval. The two women, both respected for their savory meat pies and variations of lavender honey cake, are the backbone of not just the manor but the village that surrounds it. I'd known the cooks somewhat, as everyone knows to befriend anyone with access to food. No one asks about the source of the meat in their pies. Luckily, Nannie makes everything taste good.

To Nannie, whose voice is often hushed, the best appearance of a woman is demonstrated by the cleanliness of her apron and the hem of her skirts, though to me, Nannie appears to do what she can to be invisible. Aldy's loud, trilly voice garners much attention by the other women, augmented only by her occasional and deep-chested laugh. And when she laughs, Nannie cringes and shuts her eyes tight. Not because the laughter is a bad thing but because Nannie is a worrier. In her scowl she would remind us that any attention drawn by sound or sight is dangerous for a woman. I think the women are close because Aldy likes the attention as much as Nannie prefers none of it. And by the look of it, tonight's events are not the kind to draw attention to until we are far away from the mischief.

"You're weary tonight, Mistress Dedham," Aldy says. "Well, more than usual."

Nettie shoos away her concerns.

Nannie takes bread out of the basket she carries, tears a piece off and then passes the rest of the loaf around. Aldamara gives a satisfied grunt as she bites into the bread. After a time, she says, "Ah, the same dough that makes our hot cross buns. Remember when we were young and ate them with warm mare's milk?" This produces a small smile from Nettie.

Some hours later, when we're all complaining about our tired arms and backs, Aldy lifts her chin, smooths her sleeves, then climbs to a patch of higher ground and says, "I composed a story that speaks to the evil of these times."

Someone shouts, "Okay then, go on." All of us stop what we're doing. Passing the jug, our hearts are stirred with thoughts of overcoming the injustices of the fence by those who wish to see common lands eradicated for their own gain.

The head cook of Odebury loves an audience and raises her kirtle to her calves. She clears her throat, swallowing hard, and says to all who will listen, "The lands weren't enough for the men in robes who dedicate themselves to the ways of God. Not content with the old rents, made from the sweat of our backs, the blood of our blisters, no! They bring their sheep to wallow in the fields. Sheep everywhere. More sheep than people. Let's hear you, a hue and a cry – *oioioio* – all a'yers!"

We all call out, "Oioioio!"

The rest of us begin to clap to keep the rhythm. "The

sheep that bear wool from soft bellies are, in truth, wolves that devour boy and girl alike. They stop the course of planting, destroy what was, one by one. They swallow the vine-o, they swallow it up so that all that's left is a pained heart and an empty stomach, Oh!"

"Oioioio!" We all cry in response.

The clapping stops. Aldamara lifts a shovel high toward the heavens. "Calling to our familiar spirits – hear us! Will you grieve us when we've been swept away by the army of wolves that denies the health of the land? Or will you help us nigh?"

Everyone gives another *oioioio* and gets to their feet, grabbing lanterns and digging implements designed to upfence the land that stretches well out before us. Nettie and I use mallets to uproot some of the more unyielding hedges. Sometimes, the fence comes up easily, sometimes not.

We find our way to the edge of the woods, and Nettie says that the fencing extends into them. "They are taking the mighty oaks and the streambeds for themselves, enclosing the land."

"What, why would anyone do that?"

She doesn't answer.

Suddenly, we hear the clank of metal sounding from the eastern sky as if the sunrise has summoned a battle as it climbs above the horizon. All of us look at one another and agree, unsaid, that we must abandon the work, even though there still lies a lone hedge yet to be uprooted. I smile at the women around me. We have caused enough mischief to send a message. I pray that the person who owns these lands will someday know that his thievery will not go unpunished.

Nannie and Nettie run to the woods to hunt for early morels. So comfortable are they to roam the forests when the rest of us are fearful to tempt trouble when the scars of punishment still burn. I hear laughter as the women vanish into the deep of the oaks beyond the new upfenced lands.

EXETER AND HOLTSWATER, EARLY SPRING

My knees are muddy and cool, wet from the ground soaking through my skirts and my stockings. The hill we are on is just outside of Exeter's east gate. I lie upon a blanket made of new grass and purple clover, but the moisture soaking everything is slow to dry from the recent rains.

Jack takes the bonnet off my head to which I immediately react, still so self-conscious by my short celery-shaped tresses that erupt in all directions. He sets a saddle bag down, his day's foraging of the woods nearby, mostly spring morels. I am impressed he knows where to look.

"Will you recite me a poem, writ only for me?" he asks.

"Is June in my head and July in my loins? Are the fruits of my labors September's yield and dreams fulfilled? With you, they will be, love. I am a servant of your love. The boat of bliss swells higher and higher. Meet it with a kiss."

"How fortunate I am for my birthday is in June. Tell

me more of this month, love." My eyes are closed, and my mouth is wet as the words fall from me like water in a graceful cascade of adoration. I speak these words so that my lover will heed my desire, but can I live on words forever as if they were food? Is this what life offers that fulfills me thus?

"*June may be the deceiver of the laws of nature; Is everything born to die? Or is it a moment of hope, a small window wherein it holds the year's laughter when the climbing rose and honeysuckle leave me undone? For the dreamers, hope remits the breath of last year's bloom that may return to me again.*"

He gathers me in his arms. After a moment, when the echoes of my voice have distilled into the nearby sounds of birds and the distant nicker of a horse, he says, "Would you like to know a secret? Speak to anyone about the month of their birth, and they will trust you sooner."

"So, you must trust me beyond all measure."

"Aye, love, I do."

The fatigue in my leg muscles feels well-earned. I bid Jack Straw good day and go home and fall asleep to the sounds of birds singing. Is it night or day? I awaken and realize it is still night and that Isca is not beside me. I dress and find that Hamlyn is not at home either. I head out the door.

As I go to the dairy to ask if anyone has seen Isca, Hamlyn appears walking quickly toward me just as I reach a fog-filled street near home at daybreak. He tells me Isca did not come home from the dairy. He adds, "She may have had a visit with Bessie Dunlop even though it wasn't her delivery day."

He seems disoriented. I tell him I will head up to Steepcote Hill. The shadows of the streets are lifting and the sounds that echo against the buildings are distant voices, unfamiliar. Birdsong begins in the distance, just when climb the hill to Bessie's house. A neighbor I recognize with a tall hat tells me Isca and Hamlyn are both safely home.

I enter the apartment and hear Isca crying, "I will be a good girl, Uncle!"

Hamlyn is beside himself. "This is exactly what I was fearful about! No more magic nonsense."

"But even you said the fairy people were real. Even you tie ribbons to the hawthornes… "

"The fairies can't protect you from the authorities and the church that funds them. Isca, Isca. You have no idea how you have skirted the edges of true danger. I might have lost you."

We sit in silence. Hamlyn paces the room and I can tell he debates what he should say. He tells us that this time the fine for her transgressions was higher, but by the grace of heaven, the charges were dismissed. The dairy owner agreed to provide them the money. Hamlyn asks me to speak reason to her and he leaves with his coat and a slammed door.

I don't know what I should say to her to convince her to be more careful. I was told that Isca was caught making magic by singing in Latin to the trees. We've all heard of the women being forced to confess to crimes of witchcraft. I'm not sure what got her free of being tried and ultimately convicted. Was it Hamlyn's good standing or the dairy owner's money?

She cries. She tells me that they searched her entire body, and she cringes in shame in memory of it. They found nothing but a freckle. It wasn't raised like a teat, so therefore, it wasn't a worrisome symptom in use by the devil, they said.

"There was more than one who searched you?"

"There were three men. The constable, an ugly friar, and the Holtswater priest. I recited my prayers to them, and the priest asked me how much coin could I provide."

"What did you say to that?"

"I don't have silver for them. My wages go to Hamlyn. Hamlyn came with three shillings and brought me home." Isca begins to vomit. I run to bring her a bedpan. "Will Bessie Dunlop be all right? The constable inquired about her, too."

She is worried for what she might have told them about Tom, who still lives in a milk bottle. She sits and stares away into infinity for a long time and does not respond to any of my affections or botched humor. She blinks but says nothing.

I sing a little song, *'Baa Baa Black Sheep...'* but she is still so far away from me. After a moment or two, I fall silent. And then I start again: *"All is well and shall be well..."* At first, she blinks, then turns her gaze to me. The tears come with the laughter. "Oh, Tildee, you're doing it all wrong." She sings it correctly. We sing it over and over together and it becomes a round, sweet melodies that are like tendrils of a small weeping willow arms enclosing us

111

in a summer afternoon of golden light.

She asks if she can come with me to the glade where Jack and the camp men reside. I don't tell her the whole truth of our plans and my involvement with the rogue women. I tell her my love is with Jack, and day has become night, and night has become day when I am with him. There is no time to consider life outside of our lovemaking. She delights in this and encourages us in our tryst.

TIVERTON RUINS

I maintain my work at the dairy, but as often as we can, Jack and I go further into the countryside where the world is ours to share with the unstifled cries of our desires and the discovery of what the body can procure for the soul.

One afternoon, we lie naked and perspiring on a blanket on a high hill, overlooking Exeter's radiant spires rising in the distance. The air is soft and warm. Green like the color of sea foam is everywhere. The slant of light long in the dying day rushes towards us. We look up at the heavens with the spirit of the growth all around us as if we were gods reawakening the world through the actions of our love. I hint at a life beyond the dairy.

"Mathilde, my rebel rose, where should we go?"

I had been thinking of that very thing. "We could join the mummers and live alongside a troupe, playing for tavern and manor. Can you sing? Could you be a player?"

Jack tries not to laugh and says, "No. Neither of those things."

"But you speak such eloquent words to me…"

"It is the charm that I use to find my way through the marrow of living a day-to-day existence."

"I could teach you."

"Ha!"

"Jack, I can write but can't perform. You, as handsome as you are, delivering my words through your mouth would captivate anyone. Here, try my words: *I would listen to the birds at night if they told me where to find you. I would seek the moonlit leaf if it fed me breadcrumbs of silver light to your house.*"

"I can't recite all that." We sit in the silence that we own together. "Are you always writing sonnets?"

"It is better than the storm clouds of worry in my head." I laugh and then add, "You have inspired me to answer the call, to write again."

"What worries would you have, Milady?"

"A woman alone?"

"You are not alone." He kisses the inside of my wrist. "We will build a world together. With my men and your ability to coax words out of the air...maybe we should return to visit Derbyshire." He sees that my mind is elsewhere and adds, "Lady, the shivering leaf feeds me breadcrumbs..."

I laugh without reserve.

He tells me there comes another opportunity for the rogue women to strike. I tell him I would rather be by his side for a few more hours instead. I have thought about the night of the upfencing as an invigorating exercise, but I did not find satisfaction in it as an act of vengeance. There must be other ways to put the anger related to the thieving priest behind me. Plus, I learned that the Commonwealth arrived soon after our event, and one or two of the women were arrested. After proving to myself that I may have a habit of losing places to inhabit, I don't think I want to risk more accusations and tempt the Fates anon. I don't wish to be punished my whole life.

My lover looks me in the eye." My mother once told me to honor the lady who makes the sun shine." He holds my hand." I have never met such a woman, or perhaps I am only now paying attention. Until today."

Jack gazes out across the hillside as if he is considering the different roads away from here. His eyes are searching. Then, curiously, he sighs. After a moment he practices some of my poetry that he has tried to memorize. The laughter, the playfulness erupts from our hearts over and over. Such tender moments are no longer fragile eggs that crack, no longer sharp edges of shells that cut at my insides. That timeworn bird has flown, and there is now a dove cooing in its place.

Jack asks me to wait for him, and he leaves. He is gone for hours and I become worried. Normally our trysts have been seamless, meeting within minutes of the chosen time and place. It is growing late in the day when he returns, the sky violet and the air carrying cooler pockets of a breeze. A star alights in the east. Because I am alone, I turn to leave for home, and then I see him. He is riding a horse and brings another alongside by holding onto the reins.

I raise both eyebrows. "Where are we going?" He doesn't answer; just hands me the black strip of well-worn reins to the other horse, a gelding.

I study Jack's mount and am taken aback. It has a star on its forehead and a very dark forelock. It is a tall horse he calls Dazzler. The horse looks familiar to me, somehow. The marks on his forehead and the way his head and neck collect in such a regal posture are compelling. Though the horse has been trained, it shows a fierce desire to run at full gallop at any given moment by the way he prances as if aching to go more quickly.

I approach him, first patting Dazzler's neck. I see Jack's lip is bleeding! His eyebrow is cut. And his clothes are torn. He's breathing heavily. "Let us away," he says in a strange tone, urgency just beneath his words. He promises to tell me later what has happened.

Jack tells me that mine is an eight-year-old, dappled gray and white with tender eyes. I wear skirts but can easily ride full saddle, something I learned a lifetime ago from the stable hand at Oak Hill. But I am thankful for the gentle spirit of this one.

We ride to one of Jack's encampments in the woods outside of Exeter. This is different from the camp I've been to before. This one was once part of an earl's estate, or so's the story behind the fallen stones. Most everything is gone, and only a few broken walls remain. There is an overgrown bracket of thorns and vines that encircle us and wrap around everything that was once here: the chimneys, one or two remnants of doorways made of wood. Still, there is some overhang to find shelter within. He lets me tend his wound and assures me he is okay but begs off having to tell me how he got this way. He says he is so tired he must rest. Sleep eventually arrives for us, although it takes a while to finally succumb to the quiet and the dark. The tiny fire we kindle inside a circle of old bricks is mostly smoke.

The hour grows late as we sit together. We talk of more of his plans for what the Commonwealth calls the *commotion of rebels*. I scoff at his brave intentions. To me, they are foolish.

He asks, "Would you tell me all that you have done and justified to earn a loaf of bread?"

"No, I would not." My spine straightens.

"My family fought during the Battle of Wedmore near Somerset."

"I have heard of those battles made famous by Alfred the Great, who defeated the Viking army," I say. Jack gives me a quick nod.

"My family was part of the Viking Army."

"Oh."

"My family tells tales of their adventures, mighty men and women sailing rough seas and coming to this land to make a home. I remember these stories since I was a wee cherub. But the stories are becoming forgotten. They have never been written down. There is no landmark or statue to honor them. Though they swore allegiance to the king and were baptized," he leans towards me a little, "we kept many of our heathen ways."

"Such as?"

"Well, children belonged to their mothers. Or they used to."

I grow quiet at this revelation.

Jack touches my hand. "Your ability to read and write is a rare and beautiful gift from the gods. To keep stories alive in our lifetime, they must be compiled on paper. It is no longer enough to share the stories of lives long gone with children who remember less and less."

Jack tells me he never learned to write. It's not such an uncommon occurrence for many of us, I know. He asks me if I would write his story one day. Instead of answering, I ask where his family is from.

"Heathwood near Derbyshire. I go to visit cousins that still reside there." He closes his eyes. "I can see the trees that hug the narrow street and hear the wind start. It is like a tenderness that blows along your backside as if to give you a simple nudge."

"Why, Jack, I think you could be a poet yet. Let's go there someday."

I awaken to the sounds of shouting. Torches and men everywhere in the dark suddenly appear, coming through the woods towards us.

Jack jumps up and shouts, "I thought we were ahead of them. God's teeth!"

I cannot contain my exasperation. "You were being hunted, and you didn't tell me?"

117

Jack grabs me by the arm." Go, take Dazzler. They will chase you, but they will not be able to overtake you. Go!"

I am pulled away from the firelight into the night and swallowed by the shadow of trees. Trembling with fear, he shoves me roughly in the direction of the horses. He untethers his horse and hands me the reins and the roping, no time to remove it. He shoves a drawstring duffel bag into my hands. Men shout at him, coming for him. Jack Straw stands watching me and ignoring the ten men, all hired thugs that surround him, the lights of the torches gathering in a sweep of fire, a circle of entrapment. They spot me on the dark horse and I whisper to it as I squeeze my knees, and it bolts out of the woods like no mount I've ever ridden. I hear the bright clank of metal as I ride away.

I ride at full gallop for miles. Dazzler leaps over stone and stream without a break in his stride. If anyone was chasing me, they have given up.

I am still holding on for dear life. It seems the more I pull on the reins, the faster he will go. I nuzzle my face into his mane, long and full like Nettie's old braid but black as December rain.

BLESSED COMFORT

The night has retreated, and a pale gray-yellow emerges beyond the trees. Dazzler does not appear ready to stop. I pull on the reins but to no avail; he is determined to make his way. I try not to panic. I've found myself on a runaway horse before, but they normally tire out sooner. I have lost my head kerchief, and God knows what else on this ride that will never end. I lean my head against his neck and grab the mane. I close my eyes and feel the rhythm of this beast beneath me. I feel that this horse is running as if it were going home.

After what must be over an hour of a hard gallop, I smell what is familiar. We have entered a new part of the wood near a mossy streambed. Dazzler has jumped three streams, a rocky bank, not slowing even once until finally, we are in the field west of Oak Hill. I can't see much in the dissolving darkness. The sun, newly born low within the trees, has yet to alight upon the stables, larger than I remember. I pat Dazzler's neck and say out loud, "Welcome home, Starry Boy." Mother Abbess's own horse.

I dismount at the entrance of the barn. No one is about. I feed Starry Boy oats and lead him to the water trough. I debate what to do next.

I look toward the woods, a picture upon the tranquility behind the silent walls of Blessed Comfort. The light is slanted, low gold fingers touching the verve of early green, fern, and nearby the mossy stone drawing glimmers from a creek. The water is still high from the winter storms. I can see the roof of the woodcutter's house. Nettie's presence resonates in the wood, and suddenly the memory is revealed.

A voice inside me. Nettie's voice, saying, *You have lost a part of yourself. Come back here to find the whole of you.*

Her words sound in my ear and fill me with fear and encouragement at once. This will be a wonderful story to share with her, how the fastest gelding of Oak Hill was brought accidentally home. I rub my eyes. I sense the spirit in the woods, the hue of dewy wetness that charges the light within each leaf and vine.

I sit down hard on the ground when two women from the abbey pause near the front of the barn. I press my ear to the boards of the stall.

A woman speaks. It is the Mother Abbess, and she sounds agitated. "A band of them collected in the night and destroyed the now private lands of the church of Dorset."

Another woman says, "They were but a nuisance compared to the camp men who terrorize the countryside. What a shame –"

Mother Abbess interrupts, "Idiot women, what were they thinking would happen? Would the soil stuck to their thin kitchen slippers miraculously be removed? Now that our guard is thrice times reinforced would they not be noticed coming home drunk and laughing at sunrise, aligned with the same mischief as our neighbors in Odebury?"

Another sister of the abbey comes running into the stable. She whispers to Mother Abbess, who responds, "Are you sure she is dead?" The woman nods. The three depart, back up the hill towards the convent.

Who is dead?

While walking away I hear one of the nuns ask, "What of the injured rebels?"

"Those who survive will face charges."

I run along the walls where the convent meets the woodlands and steal into the narrow room of the infirmary. Sheets are draped over two bodies laid flat, side-by-side, on a table. Candles are everywhere, and the smoke of frankincense is thick. I breathe into my hands for a moment to keep from coughing.

I see her long braid escaping the sheet.

Like falling ivy reaching out to me.

I do not need to know who lies in wait to be buried. Oh, my sweet Nettie, the only woman who offered me a gentle hand while I was growing up. I approach the table. I lift the sheet and look at her still, solemn face. Not sure how it could be more at peace than when she was living, but the lines on her face appear unburdened by worry. I cover her again and then reach my arms and torso across her body. I do not care if my tears will stain the coverlet.

There are recent blood stains marking the sheet of the body lying next to Nettie. I surmise they must have both died recently and near to one another. I pull back the sheet. It is Nannie, one of the cooks of Odebury who I last saw during the night of the upfencing.

"I wondered who had returned my stolen gelding." Mother Abbess resembles an angel from on high as she stands in the doorway, carrying a torch as the light of the hall in the background surrounds her like a halo. "I will take it as a token of good faith and not have you arrested for coming back to this property. You may have a hot meal and say a prayer for the dead before you go."

"Thank you, Mother."

I wish she had said nothing more. I wish I had run from her then because my life would be different now. But instead, she fills my head with doubt. "Did you know that your lover informed the Commonwealth of the rogue women's designs as a diversion in order for his own plan to be successful?"

I want to shout that she is lying, but instead, I run to her, as much to stop her words as to beg her to tell me everything. I fall on my knees at her feet. She says with bland coolness, "You think that we behind these walls do not know what occurs elsewhere? You think we do not know how to watch the trickery of a clever man? Especially one who steals my horse?"

HOLTSWATER

We heard rumors that Jack was taken to the Tower at London. He has become the subject of conversations in all of Exeter, stories circulating that he was one of the more infamous leaders of a ruthless brigand of rebels, one of the last of those fighting against the removal of the common lands. The sheriff and his soldiers, men of the Commonwealth, arrested over half of the rebels. Many were killed the same night as Nettie and Nannie, who were caught in the melee. Nettie had been badly injured tending to a wounded rebel on a hill near Meath and died after being brought to the abbey along with young boys fighting from both sides who had family in the area. Nannie had been killed while standing next to her own large black pot when the Commonwealth raided the woodlands.

I am overcome by moments of sadness over Jack. How can I ever believe in another person the way I allowed myself to trust Jack? Is this what love is? First affection and then betrayal? Did he truly love me? Or did he decide in those final hours together that he would keep me by his side and alive? Confusion competes with rage. Oh, if only his actions were as clear as the rich tone of his voice, like a cavern in the earth who learned to sing, and the softness of his gaze. He sacrificed his own freedom for mine. I turn these thoughts over and over again like an apple that is partially bruised but still edible.

I keep to myself in those days after the suppression of the rebels. I notice, too, that Hamlyn acts very alert and excitable, startling at every strange noise coming from the street. But no one has yet come knocking on the door looking for him. Every day, we fear less and less that he will be sought out, tried, and convicted. Some of Hamlyn's old friends, like Kurt, begin to come around, but the talk is more about what happened on that night in April than whispered discussion of future uprisings. Kurt has a license to cut wood from the nearby forest, and we've become one of his regular stops.

Life begins to return to something like it was before. Hamlyn no longer hosts meetings. Isca keeps her eyes pointed towards the ground. She and I attend church and make sure our hair is combed, and bonnets are pinned correctly.

With two shillings saved from what I earned at the dairy, I purchase a few small sheets of parchment and a new raven quill to commit the words to pages. I store them beneath the floorboard. I mix wine, rainwater and oak gal to make ink but rarely do the words stick to the parchment. One day I come home and see Hamlyn has bought a small vial of gum resin to enhance the texture of the homemade ink so that it will not run as thinly.

Perhaps someday, it will be a compilation of a new little book. I will call it *The Gift of Adoration*. I write all that I can remember of those afternoons of soft light and bare caresses. Though at times conflicted, I pour out my thoughts of those moment on the hillside outside of Exeter where the only sounds were a murmuration of pleasure and a future life together. And then sadness, more than anger, makes me succumb to a different kind of writing, a mourning of sorts. A somberness imprints upon the words that echo the realities I face.

I consider dressing as a monk, partly because I feel that clergy may have an easier time going through the world than would this dairy girl. Finding a buyer for my pages as a clergyman would be simpler than a lone woman attempting such a thing. Wearing a robe and mantle, though, would be more difficult now that my breasts are fuller. I could crop my hair and rub soot on my chin and walk in the manner I once watched Roberto walk. But instead, my work at the dairy increases.

The owner of the dairy tells us that we need to begin regular trips to deliver cream to Oak Hill. The Blessed Comfort's cow has died and the nuns of the abbey plan to use a small gift of land to raise goats and sheep. I dread the thought of walking up the narrow path to the foreboding wide wooden doors to deliver waxed covered milk tins. I mention this to Hamlyn who gives a nod. He knows that I was banished from the convent in what feels like ages ago. And the way is long for a regular delivery.

Once weekly, Hamlyn helps Isca carry cream by driving her down the little road from Holtswater to Oak Hill. I sit and wait with my monk's hood safely over my brow. As we ride, I watch the light alongside the trees and witness the plentiful rest that will come of these dark months. Those night hours will beckon to me like portals displaying vivid portraits of a story or a rhyme, inviting ideas into my mind. The ache in my belly forces me to focus instead on the mending that can be accomplished and the oils that need to be pressed to prepare for the angry cold that will soon penetrate my calloused hands. I think of Nettie and begin imagining what will be needed to grow a garden of herbs.

One afternoon, I am waiting for both Hamlyn and Isca with the horse near the wide convent doors. Over the course of the late summer months, Hamlyn began to wait with me less and less and assist Isca as she ran up the small white stone lane to make her cream delivery to the nuns of Blessed Comfort.

My neck starts to itch. It is probably from the coarse wool of the shawl I am covered up with. I worry that Hamlyn and Isca are taking too long to return to the cart. I consider leaving, old fears rising about being spotted where I no longer belong. Finally, as twilight comes, I hear the titter of Isca's laugh. The purple sky surrounds three people approaching the cart. I consider hiding but then realize the third person is Aldamara Bentley, one of the cooks from the upfencing. She walks at a prance down the hill to greet me.

Her body towers above mine as I step out of the cart.

She pulls me into an embrace and cradles my head in her arms. "Dear one!" After a few moments of heartfelt reunion, Aldamara tells me that she is now the convent cook and was hired in the days after the commotion of rebels.

The Lord of Odebury packed and left for York with his wife and entourage. Aldamara said she was lonely in the kitchens without Nannie and only a few freemen still on the lands. She brags that with only one prepared meal of duck and blackberry sauce "and the sure complement of Nannie's shepherd's pie, Mother insisted to her staff she was tired of gruel and needed someone who would be able to help properly host frequent visits from important people from Rome." She glances towards me. "I don't think anyone has had the privilege of welcoming a dignitary from yonder distance!" We laugh. Then, a strange but wonderful thing happens. Aldamara gazes deeply into Hamlyn's eyes, and he touches her forearm in a way only lovers do. Lovers who have dwelt in the comfort of each other's embrace for some time.

DEVONSHIRE, JUNE

Under an egg-shaped moon, near the river Exe, below a wide-open twilight sky, I officiate the wedding of Aldamara Bentley and Hamlyn Clemens. Nothing interrupts the arch of the heavens. The stars shimmer, and the moon courts the water like a silver cloak. We decorate an abandoned carriage house with flowers for a makeshift arbor for the ritual. I see many friends of Hamlyn's who

I've met before. Hamlyn assures me that to make it official, they would, on the morrow, seek out a priest who could present them with a license for their marriage.

Aldy's friends have fashioned wreaths made of different flowers for me and Isca. Someone brings me a scalloped robe of red and white that clasps shut just under the bosom. It looks a little worn, patched, and mended in places around the elbows and collar, but it feels sumptuous on my body, heavy in fabric, with panels of velvet, official for the rites. Aldamara is fitted with a circlet, a green gown, and surcoat. Hamlyn comes wearing a handsome coat, also borrowed from friends, that encircle us in our ceremony. Aldy and Hamlyn asked me to write their vows, and this is what I offer them to say to one another:

> *We are both metal, hard steel, defiant*
> *But soft as a petal, I open to you*
> *In trust and love*
> *That feeds what is*
> *The rarest of things one finds in this world*
> *Like a jewel but rarer still*
> *Someone you can show the whole of yourself to*
> *I love you, and I take you as my spouse*

I weave their hands together in an ancient custom Nettie once spoke about: handfasting. I bless them both using long red ribbons while spools of clouds sift across the night sky.

I do not tell them that they were words I once wrote in hope of a future with Jack Straw. That these vows were

127

part of a little book of everything I love and the poetry of a heart that suffers such unspeakable gladness and despair. For him. And now, they will be shared to honor the dreams of other lovers. And the book will remain safely under the floor.

One night, after sunset falls late in the evening, being so close to midsummer, I see the moon's fullness rising as the sun sets. It is a peculiar time, a time Nettie called the *weird hour*. An hour that beckons, an hour that the common folk remember. An hour that many of privilege ignore. As we sit at the banks by the river Exe, wringing out our clothes, we sing. All the grasses and the woods nearby yearn for the fullness of the season. Everything comes alive. The women near us join our song.

HOLTSWATER

In the days that follow, Aldamara is less with us and more often at the kitchens of the convent. We see her when we can. There is sadness in Hamlyn and perhaps Isca and I as well. Our little home, small as it is, alights by her laughter and our hearts are warmed whenever she is with us.

One night, late, Hamlyn returns home with a worried look. He removes some greens from a sack collected while at the market and places the bunch on the table in the kitchen nook. He hands me a handful of carrots and early blackberries. I pass to Isca the berries who sits next to the hearth. She looks up from mending the hem on her dairy frock and shoves a handful of berries into her mouth.

Hamlyn has news. It is the only time I can recall that he has more information to share than Isca.

"Bessie Dunlop is dead."

Her face searches Hamlyn's. She stops eating. He tells us people at the market are whispering. "That there was an argument between you and Mistress Dunlop."

Isca is silent, but her eyes say everything. "And that led to her dying?"

"Some say you poisoned her, and she fell down the stairs."

"Uncle, will they come for me?"

"I do not know."

"I was cross with her. I made her swear not to tell the dairy owner."

"Tell the dairy owner what?"

"About Tom Leaf!" Hamlyn is confused.

Her words fall stale like aged crumbs on the dusty floor as we wait for her to explain. "I bade Tom, leave her and come to me. Bessie knew I would befriend Tom once she had her proud son home again. When I took back the dairy milk bottle, I befriended Tom. I gave myself in friendship to Tom. And he was devoted to me." After a moment, she sighs, "Oh, what have I done to bring such illness upon us that I believed was goodness?"

We all stand silent, the words ringing loud as church bells. Finally, Hamlyn says, "Who is Tom Leaf?" Isca weeps into her hands. Hamlyn grabs her by the wrist and says, "You are like a daughter I never had. I have worried about you every minute since my sister left this world. The worry sets the stones under the earth to shake and the wood of the house to moan. Isca, you are all that is left from everyone I've ever loved and known and trusted. You must tell me everything because I swear I will lie down in the road to die or lie in hell in order to save you."

Well, we are all crying by now. My love for Isca and for Hamlyn knows no bounds, tis true. After we calm, we sup and go to bed early. I almost run into the street trying to escape from the wild and unrelenting thoughts in my head.

We go about the day and night that follow as normally as we can. It is the time of the year when the water of the Exe is still high. We take Hamlyn's horse and cart, bring almost all our clothing, and beat it against the rocks with a bucket of ashes and fat. A few other women, wet to the elbows and to the knees, give barely a brief nod. They know what we are about but they give us our peace as we wring the trousers and linen shifts from the cold waters. Our hands are bright pink and burning when we head home. The gossipers whisper and point when Isca and I pass through the market. Sheba moves so slowly. The clop-clop of her hoof beat rings so loudly it is like a drum to call the crowds.

The parish priest is waiting for us when we get home.

I begin to tie up the clothing to dry near the hearth. The wash is still sopping and I put a bucket below the wettest of the clothing, still dripping. The priest has a kindly look but as I watch him I see that he acts like someone in the cautious practice about to ensnare a small animal. He speaks calmly toward all of us. I am convinced that if Hamlyn wanted to stop him, Isca could run away quickly.

The priest says she must come with him now. She asks if she can bring her threadbare blanket to wrap around her instead of the old, worn cloak that needs three new patches. The young priest nods. He and Isca are near to the door when I grab her hand and hug her tightly. I feel the panic rise in both of us. They go. I stand at the shutters and watch them turning away from our street. They are met by the new sheriff, who is walking beside two other men I don't know. Hamlyn calls me back to the fire, and we contemplate what may become of her.

He stirs the pot that is hung above the dying coals, two-day-old stew with last year's turnips. I have bread that we roast over the fire. It is black and crisp in places, but it tastes fresh in the center. I wipe the soot from the crust.

"I've warned her and warned her. How do you protect a child who has no sense of danger?" We sit in the quiet and sup. Outside, a woman begins yelling, and from further away, a dog begins to bark. Another hound answers. The light of the fire is almost gone. The dark has taken all but the coals at the bottom of the hearth. We say good night and take our rest.

EXETER, MAYOR'S HALL

The court date comes.

Years earlier King Henry IV endowed Exeter with a charter that proclaimed it to be a city in its own right. It could conduct its own judicial proceedings without interference from the royal court. Exeter now elects mayors and sheriffs as well as its own coroner.

Adjacent to the market, where I was reunited with Isca, while standing in the audience watching the morality play last winter stood the Exeter Guildhall. It was rebuilt in recent years from a small, thatched toll house to an edifice fit to hold the hundred or so council members who meet regularly, as well as larger assemblies, including trials that allowed the public to watch proceedings from the gallery.

Checkerboard patterns in flint and freestone stretch across the front of the building. It reminds me of the newer parts of the monastery at St. Nicholas's. Stained glass windows, panels of the saints in frosted hues of blue and yellow with large imposing hats, curtain the north wall behind the dais where three lofty judges will look down on all of us. A wood-paneled long bench is installed around the entire room. Hamlyn and I stand at the back. He leans over and tells me that only the most skilled craftsmen, like masons and carpenters, were paid for the work of the new building. He and his friends who carted supplies to and from the construction were never compensated other than with an occasional meal.

The hall is packed with people, merchants I recognize, monks who know me. I think I espy Saul among them. He still has a halo of grey hair and dark wool robes. There are very few women, if any. I think I am allowed here because I call myself Isca's kin. The air is tight, and even though it is overcast outside, inside, we all sweat.

We are shaking, Hamlyn and I both, like children who must face their parents' judgment for not completing their chores. There is no one high-born to speak for Isca. No one to help her prepare for this hour either. They wouldn't let us see her before the trial. I was able to deliver a fresh set of garments to her yesterday at the gaol where she is kept, but there is no sign that she received them. When she appears on the floor of the courtroom, her clothes look like pieces of a gray sail that only barely survived a storm. She stands between two large men and keeps her gaze down. She is not chained but holds her hands clasped together. Her head has been shorn unevenly. I close my eyes to this. The first affront, always, it seems, is to remind women of their vanity and humble them after.

There is too much noise in the back of the gallery to hear the proceedings, but at some point, the news reaches us that confirms Isca is on trial for the murder of Bessie Dunlop through the crimes of witchcraft. This we, of course had already heard in the streets. But our world shrinks into unbearable moments of fear now that the truth of it is real.

Guards bring Isca forward. They tell her where to stand, which is directly before the judges who loom above her like birds of prey.

The coroner speaks. It is one of the rare times during the trial when a hush falls over the room. Mistress Dunlop, he reports, was found at the bottom of her staircase. Six stairs in all. But she also appeared to have a sizeable wound on the back side of her head. He suggests that the fall could provide the most simple answer, that her tumble down the stairs was an accident, even though it is so sad and meaningless and not what the public wants to hear.

The large hall is so loud with people talking. Hamlyn and I look to one another again and again to try to discern what is being said. The only people in the room that seem to be having a conversation are the judges and the prosecutor who I can barely see but notice at one point, with a parting of the crowd at the front of the room, that he has large buckles on his boots that stomp and shake the floors. All the noise gives me a headache. Someone near me in the gallery says the prosecutor is sometimes called the *witchfinder general*.

One of the judges asks the coroner if it isn't at all possible that Isca had poisoned Bessie Dunlop with witchcraft and, therefore, she may have fallen down the stairs after becoming ill.

Isca emits a loud *tsk tsk* and crosses her arms. I can tell she wants to say something, but the judge turns and glares at her. She tries to be still but keeps moving around as if she's trying to get comfortable standing atop a broken dish.

The judges call the Holtswater priest to the stand. He talks about catching Isca stealing wafers from the church and later feeding one to her familiar. A toad.

Isca shouts, "He was hungry!" A judge scolds her for speaking out of turn.

The prosecutor speaks softly, trying to coax Isca. "Tell us about the fairies."

"I can't speak of them."

"Oh pray, why not?"

"They will abandon me."

"When did you approach them?"

I stand for a moment upon a part of the decorative oak carving that juts out of the wall near the floor. I can see her. She's annoyed, I can tell, but she flinches, keeping her head away, her eyes darting anywhere but upon the gaze of everyone in front of her. "It is commonly known that you are never to speak to them unless they address you first."

"Who?"

"The fairy folk!"

"And did they?

"Who?"

"By God, woman. The fairy folk. Did they approach you?"

After a moment. "Yes, sir."

"When?"

"They did after many nights of me singing and praying near the hawthorn tree that grows by the cross street near our house. And to the moon when it was full."

"Is it true it was a full moon when Bessie Dunlop fell to her death?"

"I wouldn't know anything about that."

The prosecutor asks if the fairies demanded that she abandon God to garner their affection.

No one can hear her. She is muttering to herself. Finally, she gives a bleak nod. The courtroom emits a collective gasp. Silence for the next few minutes as everyone waits for the next question.

"What do they promise you in return?" Another course of silence.

"That I would never want for meat, drink, clothes, or money."

A few sputters of outrage surround us then, but when she speaks again, more loudly this time, it roils the courtroom. "Never been assured of this by God unless you count the afterlife, but I'm hungry now and tired of feeling poorly every day when my head hurts, and the townsfolk yell at me, and I've not even met twenty years."

"Tell us how they provide you with these gifts. When do you see these spirits?"

"They are not spirits, as far as I can tell. They come in my dreams, and they speak to me at night under bridges or by the water as sure as you are speaking to me now."

There is shouting from the men at the front of the room. The clergy in the corner are purple with anger, as they would be. The townsmen in my midst are accusing Isca of having demonic alliances. Some are demanding that she hangs from the gallows.

Among the accusers are two monks in brown wool robes. One is Saul, shouting his indignations. He looks as outraged as the day he expelled me from the monastery.

Isca sighs heavily.

The prosecutor asks her to talk about one of her familiars, the toad or the little man she spoke of during their inquiry of her in her recent comments. He reminds her she has confessed that she and Bessie Dunlop fought over a familiar who took the shape of a little tiny man.

In Isca's emotional state, she begins very quietly. I can see that she is scared. She's trembling and making a face I've never seen before. As if she's trying to smile and yet is in agony. She looks so small in the center of the room.

Something that the prosecutor says enrages her. We can't tell what he asked. "Gads! I was Bessie's friend, when no one else would speak to her. Yes, we loved to talk of fairies, for who else is as curious as she about what will make the fairies laugh and which treats they like best? Bessie was my friend and I shall miss her!"

The judges are men of rank. Bearded, older, they are cautious with their speech and careful with their accusations. One of the judges leans forward. The tone of his voice has noticeably changed as he encourages Isca to speak of her relationship with the fairy, Tom Leaf.

Everyone in the guildhall is now enrapt and whereas it was earlier raucous, when even the judges could barely hear one another, now all are silent and still either standing in the back of the room with Hamlyn and I or those of privilege who sit along the walls perched atop the high wood carved benches.

Isca weeps openly when describing her love of the fairies. It is as if she is speaking about a lover who has broken her heart. She only becomes more upset as she describes her relationship with Tom who joined Bessie Dunlop in lonesomeness after the years of absence of her son. Isca does not mention the milk bottle where Tom had lived in that time until Bessie's son returned. She said she demanded that it was her turn to know Tom and to love

Tom. That by all rights, she knew best how to beseech the fairies and had learned what the fairies wanted. She denies the murder and pleads for her life.

"This is blasphemous!" screams the prosecutor and the room is loud again. The clergy near the front are nodding and speaking to one another as if they are hatching a plan for Isca's doom.

When the wave of talk wanes, I can hear Isca making the smallest sounds, *cluck cluck, cluck cluck*. After her testimony, looking completely out of place in this beautiful room with stained glass windows and wide oak carvings everywhere, I wonder, how could this ever work to her favor?

Bessie Dunlop's husband stands to testify. I see him look at Isca in a way that makes my skin crawl. It is like a smile, but no, a sneer. He watches Isca when he moves to the front of the room and then nods before the judges. He reports plainly that he found his wife dead at the foot of the stairs. He points his finger at Isca and says she's to blame.

The court takes a recess, and we, among the other townsfolk, empty out of the building. In the market, there are women trying to sell me posies. She has tattered black wool wrapped around her hands. One asks about Isca. I glance away. At first, I feel compelled to tell her everything. So strange it is to collect my thoughts and

138

to not share them, telling no one about our plight. It is as if I am a hound bound in chains, kept from chasing a hare. I bite my tongue. No one in the market, at church, or passersby needs to know about our fears for Isca. But the gossip will be thick and plenty as snippets from the guildhall revelations leak into the streets.

We are about to turn for home when Hamlyn tells me he will meet me anon. He has loaned Sheba to a neighbor and will go retrieve her.

Just as I turn toward Holtswater Road, I hear a woman scream and hear the slamming of a coach wheel upon stone on the street. A horse and carriage have just run into someone who was crossing Milk Street.

I already know who it is. The white beard, the long cream shirt and tunic-length coat draw people near him. Lifeless he seems.

Hamlyn.

I cry out and run to his side. The driver of the carriage is fast beside us and begins muttering first apologies then complaints of how Hamlyn walked right in front of him.

"Is there a physician? Help us, please!" I look around, but townsfolk shake their heads and move on toward their destinations.

Hamlyn has survived but was knocked senseless to the cobblestone street. He has a bruise or two but what seems worse is his knee. It is swollen twice as wide as it was before. He cannot bend it and so props it on the chair at home. Took what felt like twenty years to get him up the stairs to the flat.

A messenger comes to the house and brings a summons by the prosecutor who demands that Hamlyn testify in in the hall on the morrow. When we complain of Hamlyn injury, the little man in the gray coat agrees to send a carriage to collect Hamlyn. I yell after him, "And send a crutch as well!"

Aldamara comes to her beloved's side and stays with us keeping vigil over Hamlyn's health through the night. She gives Hamlyn an infusion that makes him sleepy. He begins to yawn. She tells me, "Valerian and skullcap tea." She rubs a liniment on his knee. I wonder, would Nettie do something similar? Is this one of her ointments? Once Hamlyn finally finds sleep, Aldy and I talk about our lost friends, Nettie and Nannie.

"Couldn't be more different, those two, could they?" I laugh as I swallow tears. I am grateful to Aldamara for friendship, for someone who will remember those lost as I do.

Later, when I retire to my bed, I hear Hamlyn call for Aldy. They talk late into the night.

Hamlyn arrives to court on time with Aldamara and I at his side. His limp is severe but at least he does not cry out as he did the day before. The prosecutor is not happy with another woman in the room. Hamlyn is allowed to sit down while he testifies. He leans the old wood crutch against his leg. He sighs deeply and answers the questions that the judges give him.

He pleads with the judges, looking directly at them as they study him from above, saying she is all the kin that he knew from his youth. He nods to Aldy and then to me, saying we are his new family, and by God's grace, we are good for one another. I swallow hard, for everyone knows about me and my punishment. Fewer know the truth of my masquerade at the monastery, and sometimes, as I've heard, the rumors are wilder than what actually occurred.

He weeps. "Isca, daughter of my sister now dead, a girl left injured by the callousness of a brick builder's negligence. To look at her is proof that evilness does not explain her. She is a simple girl, after all. Please, let her come to me, and I will keep her from harm. I will keep her close and never let her fall away from God's work."

The court is silent. They want to believe Hamlyn.

Bessie's son takes the stand. He wears a uniform, having become a yeoman of the guard after fighting in a battle against the rebels two summers ago. He is now respected by both sheriff and nobility. Everyone actually. He commands attention. Insignia of thistle and rose are embroidered across his knee-length scarlet coat. His face is solemn beneath the wide-brimmed black hat that matches his stockings and buckled shoes. He is very fancy indeed.

Isca is innocent, he insists. He tells a different story than what has been circulated on the streets, than what is argued by the prosecutor. He says that Isca befriended his mother and never betrayed the friendship, even after a quarrel he overheard after returning home from serving his king. He knew the trouble that fairies caused and believes that Tom Leaf and a host of demons at first entertained but then caused a spell of confusion upon both women. Obviously, he said, women are more susceptible to this confusion than men, as it has been argued now since the time of the Greeks.

Those dressed in ecclesiastical robes who sit near the front at a place of honor sneer from this testimony. James Dunlop continues, "The fairies are stories that the women told one and another. And their argument on the day in question has more to do with a lost milk bottle that my mother has stubbornly refused to return to the dairy owner."

I look at Hamlyn, and he to me because we both knew what the milk bottle represented to Isca and to Bessie. But apparently, the son does not. The son continues, "The dairy master is in the gallery. Let him attest to this."

Of which he did. We could not tell what the prosecutor asked James Dunlop or the dairy owner, but everyone shifts uneasily, appearing more irritated by this turn of events, especially the judges who sit back in their chairs grumbling.

The prosecutor tells Bessie's son he may go.

James says, "I have one more thing to share."

He says something to the court, two of the judges watch him closely as he speaks. The third is looking down at his parchment, the trial documentation. Bessie's son says he saw his father hit his mother on more than one occasion and once came home drunk, swinging a mallet around coming closer and closer to his mother's head. There may have been gasps from everyone around me, but by all truth, there is no such thing as a world without women's pain. Such accounts would never deter a judge from what he might otherwise be convinced of. But coming from this man of means, perhaps this time it is different?

It is no secret that Master Dunlop drinks every night at a nearby tavern and often stumbles home. It is no secret that he yelled at his wife, though everyone pretended to not see it. No one feels encouraged to speak out on the affairs of families who aren't their own. Even if they are their own, no one speaks of how a husband treats a wife. The coroner steps forward and asks if the judges would allow it, can James Dunlop describe the mallet? The judges nod, and all gasp as James produces, from out of his coat, a wooden mallet. It has a dark stain upon its wider end. He passes the mallet to the coroner. Much is said then between those men of authority but few of us can hear what they say.

The coroner looks at the mallet, first on one end and then the other, and says to the judges this could have been used to cause the injury on the back of the head.

The coroner asks the son if he believes that Isca cursed Bessie when they argued. I don't know where the prosecutor is. Silence dominates the large room. "In truth, I think it plain that my mother fell under the bloodied mallet to her death." The coroner nods, still handling the mallet. He swings it back and forth, feeling the weight of it. I am sickened by this.

The husband, Master Dunlop, who had been standing at the front of the gallery, begins to yell at his son. The judges yell at Master Dunlop to sit down. It is becoming apparent to all of us. The town drunk holds far less esteem than a young proud member of the king's guard.

The son says, "I loved my mother. I miss her. Don't blame what came to pass on a simpleton who sang songs to keep my mother happy in her grief for my absence."

The elder Dunlop begins to make his way to the doors of the entrance and the prosecutor appears. Three guardsmen move quickly towards the entrance. The judges tell the Dunlop to remain where he is. Isca is no longer being charged for murder.

We try to give our thanks to James Dunlop. I run outside, cutting through the crowd of men leaving the courtroom. Bessie's son is already away. I call after him, "You saved her life, sir. We are thankful." He gives a bare wave from a coach and is gone.

I turn around to assist Hamlyn, but instead, my eyes rest on Saul, who is across the street. He shouts something. I step forward and see he is standing over a young woman who is sitting on the cobblestones with her two children. The babes are dirty. One looks as if he has a soiled bottom. She holds out a small wooden cup, begging. He glares, "You would use your own children to make fools of us all, to own our sympathies in your greedy deceits." Another monk, dressed like Saul runs from the doors to the guildhall and begins to try to calm him.

Then he turns to the mother who is now crying. "Pray, there is food offered near the fountain by St. Nicholas's. Get yourself there and have bread."

The woman slowly stands and pulls her ripped shawl closer to her shoulders. She picks up the smaller child and takes the other by the hand. She walks up the hill away from the two men of God.

We learn the following week that Master Dunlop is sentenced to hanging for the murder of his wife. The milk maids at the dairy and the blacksmith around the corner agree this is a rare thing. When Isca comes home, we stand together, our arms holding each other in a circle, and cry. Hamlyn prays that peace will follow.

Isca must wear a scold for three days. The sheriff who fits her with it calls it a *branks*. He chuckles a little when he locks it in tight, saying, "That'll keep her voice down." I have seen it used around the markets on women young and old and once at church. All women who are forced to wear these iron caps from Hell makes themselves invisible one way or another forever afterward.

At first I thought the iron frame wrapped around her head like a horse bridle would be permitted to be removed when she needed to sup, but it is even worse than that. The bridle bit that presses down inside her mouth is barbed and continually cuts her mouth and tongue if she tries to speak. Painful as it is humiliating, she carries around a small rag to sop the blood and saliva that oozes from her lips. Though the iron bars are squarely in front of her face, I help her drink some broth. Tears roll from her eyes across her temples. I wipe them away gently with a small rag. It is awkward as we spoon the liquid into the side of her mouth, but she is able to get some nourishment. When she goes out in public Hamlyn must lead her by a leash. When she first came home, she had a bell attached to the back of the thing. But Hamlyn managed to remove it.

Every morning, I say to Isca, "How fortunate you are home." I do not know how else to comfort her. I wish to tell why I believe she is lucky. The stories of England and the women hung or burned as witches are not confined to healers, though that is what plenty of the nearby housewives assert. There is constant doctrine delivered on Sundays now at the pulpit in Holtswater that declares all fairies and fairy lore is just another way the Devil is attempting to drive good people away from God. The priests never spoke of the devil in church before now.

When I was young, before I went to live with the sisters of the Blessed Comfort, I had seen a wagon drawn by two horses on the road leaving Oak Hill, and at the back of a cart, there were about dozen women standing, stumbling. Their hands bound, with hoods over their heads, they cried out in fear, falling over as the wagon tried to navigate the muddy ruts. One of the men on the bench in the front looked like he was part of the king's guard, but that was probably my childhood sense of the only authority I knew of at the time.

The man in the uniform screamed at the women to be silent.

I may never have noticed the wagon at all if I hadn't heard the crying. Begging to be released. I remember having the intense and visceral realization at that time that my own mother would never come home. The truth about the finality of death had reached my young mind.

When returning to a normal life, days after the scold is removed, I am more relieved of Isca's release than she is. She is quiet and sullen, and her anger that spikes suddenly then turns to sadness that leaves her weeping uncontrollably.

Isca tells me that she at first felt guilt at the revelation of the fairies, that their abandonment of Bessie may have been what introduced herself to danger. But what could be worse? Isca said that since she revealed to everyone all she knows about the fairies, they have abandoned her. She could no longer hear their voices, no longer fall asleep to their sweet song. She berates me as if I am a fool, "I would wear this iron bridle for one thousand days if it meant the return of my woodland friends to me." She cries herself to sleep each night thereafter for weeks.

EASTERN HOLTSWATER

November makes both a beautiful and a dreadful time.

The brown gold veins of thinning leaves enchants while I perform my daily tasks, and in turn, the slanting light calls to my heart the possibility of words to compose. I'm yearning to put feather to ink and ink to parchment and, therefore, be distracted all day. My spirit, when all is quiet, and I am alone, begs to do more than bottle milk and sleep in a bed free of lice. Isca, in a quiet moment, smiles at me and pats the seat next to her at the hearth to join her in winding rope from Sheba's horsehair and woodrushes found at the edge of the woods.

Hamlyn and Aldamara announce that they have found a home to rent on land that belonged to a nobleman but whose widow has decided to live at court in London. It is a small house of wattle and daub. It was a yeoman's house and has a chimney in the central part of the front room next to stairs for an upper floor. The whole of it smells like smoke, and there are soot stains on every wall, but it is much larger than the apartment in Holtswater and it is closer to Aldamara's work at the convent. Plus, it is far easier to keep Hamlyn's cart and horse on the land behind the house instead of on a distant street. There is a makeshift barn for hay and shelter for Sheba as well.

Hamlyn begins making plans to buy another mare or two and speaks of keeping breeding cows to use for a plow as well as for leather, meat and milk. Our chores all increase by helping to run the house, maintaining the dung heap for next year's small crop in the field, stooking hay from the meadow and regularly mending all the tools and harnesses – not to mention the clothing.

Mother Abbess had at one point insisted Aldy reside

in the small room behind the kitchens, and up until now she had spent most of her time there. Aldamara pleaded with the abbess that since she was married, and because of their new home, she wished to travel home every evening to be with her husband. Mother agreed, finally, she would be permitted to abide with her husband.

Hamlyn has plied the hearth with a new face of stonework and a proper grate to brew soups and cook meat on a spit. Aldamara oversees Hamlyn's craftwork so that more than one pot may simmer at a time. She is the best cook I've ever known. At first some dishes were what she called modest fare, though the smells of juniper mixing with meat in the large pot made my mouth water constantly. Then she began to procure what she refers to as the finer mixes and introduced us to spices like cardamom and coriander. Of late there are stews that Aldy cooks for us, often with vegetables. She infers that sometimes the cloister has plenty of food to share from the garden, especially now that the Lord and Lady of the manor have traveled north.

One night after dinner the four of us sip hot cider pressed from this year's apples—a baleful as payment in exchange for one of Hamlyn's recent deliveries. There are small shards of cinnamon sticks in each wooden cup. Aldy confides the spices are most often gotten from the convent. She admits the sisters do not eat anything beyond their bland meals, and so the spices sits untouched unless a dignitary visits. By the look in her eyes, there is more to tell. I stoke the fire, and we pull our chairs a little closer to the heat. The door is wide open to clear some of the smoke.

Aldy says in a hushed voice, "I see many things at the abbey for no one's eyes but the most private among them." I lean forward. She reveals that during the summer months while she stayed often with the nuns of the Blessed Comfort, she overheard much in the way of forbidden love between the women.

Isca runs from the room, covering her ears and shaking her head. She is convinced that all people of the cloth are beyond earthly delights. More likely, though she is still bound in fear by what happened to her in these recent months. Her hair has grown back, and she lets me braid it for her. But there is very little chatter between us. A sadness often invades her moods and rests upon her for hours. She has become more regimented than I. She tells me when my frock is pinned incorrectly when my hair needs better tucking under my bonnet. She keeps a schedule and is on time or early for everything, especially church. Every once in a while, though, at the end of the day, when the fire is low and no one is around, we sing her little song, *All is well*.

I refrain from asking Aldy how she knows about the sisters, but no matter, she cannot stop herself. She leans forward and barely whispers, "They recite verses of love to one another. They even have a favorite poem they whisper at night when all the candlelight is extinguished. The verses that they repeat are often like their own hymnal. It fills my veins with fear for them if they were ever caught. In truth, I guess nuns are mortal women just the same." Apparently, the voices often come from Mother Abbess's

150

room.

When Aldamara speaks the words of one of the poems, I spill my cider. "Their favorite appears to be the one—let me see if I can tell it right. Ah, yes, *'Why is there yearning in a woman's breast? Is it a pearl that pulses through the body in search of a lover's touch?'* "

I hold my cup steady with both hands. After a moment, I look at Aldy. I nod at both of them. "I must retrieve my book."

BLESSED COMFORT

At an appointed time in the hours after sunset we gain entrance to the inner world of the convent, a place I haven't entered in what feels like a decade. Aldamara assures me it is safe as she leads me through the labyrinthine halls. Cold floors, green glass windows. Nothing has changed. But everything is different.

We tiptoe into Mother Abbess's rooms while she is traveling, which is very rare. We waited for another moon to pass before the opportunity arose. The nuns who are not part of the entourage are in the small white chapel next door for nocturns. I have never been inside Mother Abbess's chambers before. She has small shelves with votives of the virgin and child atop a beautiful piece of embroidered cloth. There are two framed pieces of art featuring landscapes that are easily as large and impressive as those displayed in any nobleman's hall. I look quickly through drawers and under bed linens. The bed frame is of ornate wood and the bed curtains have gold threads sewn as roses along the border.

I am about to give up when I hear a noise coming from the floor below me. I look at my feet and follow my gaze. The corner of the rug is folded upward where the wooden bed posts meet a storage trunk as if it has been hastily arranged. At first I think of that long ago day when I helped Hamlyn deliver a rug to a place where I no longer belonged. And then, I am reminded of the strange little prediction that Isca shared with me months ago. I drop to my knees and look under the bed. In a basket with other small prayer volumes is my little book.

Oh, tender friend, confident of all my desires! I am overcome and begin to weep. I hold it to my chest and pet it as if it were covered in the softest fur. Some of the pages have come loose from the ribbon, tucked and folded, pulling free of the stiff cover. But the contents are otherwise intact. Aldamara calls to me in a loud whisper from outside the room. "The carriage, it returns!" I reflect for a moment and kiss my little book. A long-lost warmth fills my heart. It is the trickle of a cloaked sea of open, endless thoughts and rhymes that are mine to use. I hear a small voice inside me say, "Someday, will come new words." Without another thought, I place the book back in the basket under the bed.

We steal through the narrow halls, edging closer to the anticipated cold night air, breathing deeply. Round moons of breath-like clouds waft away from me. A sudden awareness comes, starting in my belly. It is a fire that will stoke dreams to be revealed in future pages. I stretch my arms out on either side of me, trailing my fingers along

152

the molded panel walls, old burdens lifting away, reaching more widely than I ever have before.

EPILOGUE: FROM THE DESK OF MARY CANTWELL, RESIDENT OF EXETER

My Diary,

I must remark of the day's events, for I have not seen my good husband in such glad spirits since Epiphany.

He returned home to me late after vespers. I am now three days past child bed and am hoping to return to his side presently, for his leather works are in demand and will require much of our labors.

He told me of two visitors he had today in our shoppe. As he shared his encounter, he thanked me for our supper of cold lamb mutton whilst he ate. He said it was delicious.

There was the elder, Master Hamlyn, who delivers goods with his strange ox cart and a monk. Hamlyn introduced my husband to the monk, who is tall and thin with small bursts of red hair that sprout around his head like unkempt wheat sheaves. He may be a eunuch, so tall and thin is he, with a soft, high voice like one who sings for God. They tell my dear Master Cantwell they wish for him to patronize their play, a new morality play about a woman named Nettie Dedham who, with the help of an angel named Roberto, saves an untold number of lives.

My husband asked to hear more about the play. It is commonly known that the most up-and-coming merchants of our fair city sponsor these arts and gain favor from buyer and nobleman alike. I'm sure that this is not the first time my smart husband has thought of such a thing.

The monk spoke so softly that Master Cantwell said

he had to lean in to hear his voice. The sweet refrain of a true playwright warmed his heart. "The monk said this play will take place in the merry month of May." How pleased my husband was by this.

It was as if God gave him a miracle of happenstance. My husband told him, "What a coincidence! My birthday is in May. I will gladly sponsor your play."

ACKNOWLEDGMENTS

If there is one piece of wisdom I have been fortunate enough to obtain it is that the beloved people in my life who encouraged me to keep going are the only reason this little story exists. My heart is full of gratitude to Cheryl Sadowski, Molly Dedham, Susan Weltz and Bette Siegel. Thank you for reading the earliest versions of Mathilde and her brood.

Finding friends beyond your thirties can be challenging but also offers some of the most rewarding of bonds. Thanks for feeding my headspace and my heart with powerful and inspirational possibilities. With you, the world is a better place: Ellie, Rachel, Cami, Janice, Julia, Misti, Ashley, Lynn, Domnica.

Having support to improve the craft along the way from Elizabeth Ward and Anne Brewer from Reedsy was a game changer. This proved so much more results effective than just relying on those days when I thought I might be inspired by the planets aligning and the moon waxing (although they help too...). Speaking of planets aligning, I am honored and excited to be part of the Rebel Satori Press family. Each of their publications speak "home" and "inclusion" to me.

Endless gratitude goes out to my amazing daughters who humble me with their love and to my husband, David, who encourages me to be me in all of my wild states. Finally, thanks to my Dad, John Campbell, and my sister, Kay Campbell, for our clusters of family togetherness that show proof that to write is a very normal thing and it is aligned with love.